Mrs. J. H. Riddell

The head of the firm

A Novel. Vol. 1

Mrs. J. H. Riddell

The head of the firm
A Novel. Vol. 1

ISBN/EAN: 9783337046279

Printed in Europe, USA, Canada, Australia, Japan

Cover: Foto ©Andreas Hilbeck / pixelio.de

More available books at **www.hansebooks.com**

THE HEAD OF THE FIRM

THE

HEAD OF THE FIRM

A NOVEL

BY

MRS. J. H. RIDDELL

AUTHOR OF
'GEORGE GEITH OF FEN COURT,' 'TOO MUCH ALONE,'
'FAR ABOVE RUBIES,' ETC.

IN THREE VOLUMES
VOL. I.

LONDON
WILLIAM HEINEMANN
1892

CONTENTS OF VOL. I.

THE HEAD OF THE FIRM.

CHAPTER I.

' IF TIMOTHY FERMOY.'

WHIT MONDAY, bright, brilliant—fine as fine could be !

From the London excursionist's point of view, an ideal Whit Monday !

A scorching sun to—in his own artless phrase—'bite his back,' a bitter east wind to temper the heat, dust enough to render a pause at each favourite wayside tavern not merely excusable, but necessary, plenty of company in brakes, waggonettes, spring carts, and even costers' barrows, to beguile the long way with shout and laughter, song and repartee, the unearthly noise drawn from an

agonized cornopean, or the gay and festive
tones of some wheezy concertina lightly
touched by the funny gentleman indis-
pensable to each party, capable, in his own
opinion and that of his friends, of adorning
any circle, and who meanwhile kindly delights
his own !

Never, surely, was there a finer Whit
Monday, which, after all, is *the* holiday of
the year to Londoners—the day thought of,
looked forward to, and back upon, with feelings of intense satisfaction.

On the especial Whit Monday when this
story opens, people had poured out of town
in their thousands and hundreds of thousands.
Every road leading to any place of popular
resort was alive with excursionists.

At the railway termini trains filled with
happy, eager men and women and children
were despatched to the accompaniment of
waving handkerchiefs, hearty cheers and
lusty choruses. The river steamboats were
crowded with passengers. London proper
was as a city of the dead. Shops and
offices were closed. It was possible to walk

down the middle of Fleet Street and Cheap-side—the teeming life of England's Metropolis had temporarily forsaken London, and left the great city to silence and solitude. Even in the suburbs there prevailed a quiet foreign to neighbourhoods in which tradesmen's carts usually flashed about like meteors, dashing round corners and putting timid ladies and elderly gentlemen in terror of their lives.

Noon had come and gone. It was that usually busy hour when working-class fashion ordains there shall be much running to and from adjacent bars; when children are de-spatched with jugs and bottles for a liquor which appears more to be desired than water in the desert by the arid throats of an indus-trial population; but on that fine Whit Monday there were no children left in London to run with two pennies or four pennies clasped tight in their little hands for pints or pots or any measure whatsoever.

The children were out of town, and the pennies too. The accustomed taverns were deserted in favour of more rural houses, where beer could be scarcely drawn fast enough to assuage the thirst of London on this its gigantic holiday.

In a back street of Battersea not one human being was astir. A dog, with a rusty coat and a mere wisp of a tail, was investigating the state of the gutters; on a doorstep a cat sat in the sun waiting either for the return of her family or such time as the spirit might move her to start on some marauding expedition; at one first-floor window a blackbird, with ruffled feathers, stood silent on the floor of his cage, thinking, it might be, of the woodland home he would never see again; on some of the sills protected by lilliputian railings, or greater triumphs of artistic skill, which probably gave more pleasure to their owners than deer park or chase ever conferred on a lord of the soil, bloomed gay flowers that seemed to shrink and shiver as the east wind swirled along. The silence was wonderful, and the sense of utter desolation more wonderful still.

In the heart of a populous city the absence of all sign of life affects the imagination with

a deeper feeling of loneliness than any ex-
panse of desert or wild waste of moorland, or
desolate stretch of seashore when the waves
are receding from it and night is drawing
slowly on.

About half-way up this street, which was
a thoroughfare, there turned another, which
was a *cul-de-sac*, being fenced in at the end
by a high wooden paling that the bad boys
of the neighbourhood were always trying to
climb, and where they were always coming
ignominiously to grief.

Whether the builder of this short street
lost heart, or the mortgagees prematurely
foreclosed, it is difficult to say, only one
thing is certain, viz., that the ' snug little
estate fully ripe,' *vide* advertisement, was not
developed to its full extent.

After the enterprising leaseholder had
erected twelve six-roomed houses more like
each other than peas in a pod on one side
of the road, and twelve similarly attractive
residences on the other, he broke out into
a double-fronted mansion, and then fled
either to the Bankruptcy Court or to yet

riper plots, leaving eligible sites for eight dwellings on the left and six on the right hand side vacant for someone more sanguine or possessed of a larger capital than himself to utilize.

In the neighbourhood of Battersea vacant spaces are not long permitted to lie idle; therefore, one was without delay converted into a playground for the juvenile inhabitants, and a corner where their elders beat their mats and carpets, while the tenant of the palatial mansion which boasted a window on each side of the front-door promptly proceeded to erect a lean-to against the gable of his house and boundary wall of his small yard.

The cost of this shed did not run into much money. A few lengths of 'quartering,' a good 'deal' in six-foot egg-chests, an equally admirable bargain in a lot of hemp carpeting, faded but sound, a few pounds of nails, some gallons of gas-tar, half a yard of Thames gravel, a couple of second-hand window-sashes, and behold there sprang like magic from the earth an im-

promptu greengrocer's shop and stable, both
capable of being locked up at night, and
both ' as snug as snug could be.'

When the landlord's agent saw these
architectural triumphs he accepted the position in a proper spirit and raised the rent.

It was the only thing he could well do,
for the ingenious tenant was possessed of a
strong will, a deep hoarse voice, and a lordly
temper, and though he acquiesced in the
justice of paying a trifle for the use of the
land, would have resented and resisted any
attempt to interfere with the annexe of
which he himself had been the designer and
builder.

All in good time he worked up a ' round.'
There are men in London who make a living
by getting together a connection and then
selling it. He was but a beginner—a mere
tyro—with only a set of weights and scales,
a few sacks, several bushel and half-bushel
baskets, a barrow, donkey and old set of
harness; yet for these items, his few customers, and the makeshift shed he erelong
received thirty pounds current coin of the

realm, with which he departed to work up another and better business elsewhere.

On that bright Whit Monday, though the double-fronted house was closely shut up, the door of the shop stood open.

Passing from the street, bright with sunshine, into the rude shed was like going from the light of day into some dark, cool grot; but when once his eyes became accustomed to the gloom, a person could see objects even at the extreme rear clearly enough.

In its way the store was well stocked. If it contained nothing rich or rare, there were plenty of those articles which in such a neighbourhood are always in request.

Coal and coke, of course, with bundle wood and a few ' wheels,' though the latter did not find much favour ; bins half full of potatoes ; dried herbs suspended from the roof, breathing forth, even in death, a pleasant fragrance. Spanish onions were there in sieves, and spring onions in bundles ; on a board sloping towards the window were ranged punnets filled with small salad, while radishes, round, French breakfast, and long red, blushed

crimson amidst watercresses plucked fresh
that morning from streams which trickle
slowly to the Wandle.

There were not wanting signs, either, to
prove a considerable amount of perishable
stock had been recently disposed of.

Half-bushel and bushel baskets evidently
not long previously full of green stuff stood
piled up empty. One solitary orange marked
the spot whence a goodly company of its
fellows had disappeared; not a nut, whether
barcelona, brazil, or cocoa was to be seen ;
but half a dozen shrivelled and wizened
apples were left at the bottom of a capacious
basket; quarts of unripe gooseberries had
gone to provide the necessary pudding or pie
accounted an essential dish in a Whit Sunday
dinner; only two stone bottles of ginger-beer
at a penny apiece kept each other company,
and not a lemon could have been purchased
even in exchange for sixpence current coin of
the realm.

Since the previous Friday trade had apparently prospered in Field Prospect, as the
stunted street was called. Indeed, anyone

versed in the signs which indicate failure or
success might have gathered at a glance that
trade had been good for a sufficiently long
time to justify the proprietor of such an establishment 'going out' on Whit Monday with
a clear conscience, a full purse, and a merry
heart.

Nevertheless, the owner had not gone out.
Instead, she sat among her empty baskets on
an inverted bushel measure, knitting a prosaic
stocking, and as she knit she sang, not joy-
ously, or yet with the sad song of the robin
when autumn leaves are falling and the most
mournful season of the year preaches to us of
fading life and coming death, but softly, as
one who tells some pleasing, melancholy tale
such as youth delights in, merely because
youth fails to realize that the melancholy
may chance to be all its own when the delight
has departed.

She, the owner, the singer, was young;
just two-and-twenty, with most of life pre-
sumably before, and certainly a vast amount
of sad experience behind, her.

Was she pretty ? If her features were analyzed, 'No.' If anyone took her face as a whole, 'Yes,' and much more.

Once her hair had been red — not the brilliant orange scarlet that remains unchanged till time powders it with snow, but the deeper, darker, richer red, that mellows into a lustrous brown flecked with gold as the light shifts and changes upon it.

Her skin was fair with the exceeding fairness that often accompanies hair such as hers.

Not all the long exposure to sun and rain, not the piercing north wind or the bitter east, had as yet been able to mar its pure white. She was much freckled, and her hands were browned, but in other respects she might have been sitting at ease all her life, so delicate was her complexion. Curling naturally, her wavy hair wandered in soft little ripples over a forehead which might have been thought somewhat too broad for beauty ; her mouth was large, and her nose belonged to no recognised order. Yet looking in that frank face, lit up with such wonderful eyes, who could suspend admiration in order to criticise the other features ?

Those eyes were the glory of the girl's face
—kind, good, faithful eyes, soft and tender,
of that clear limpid brown which is so seldom
seen after early childhood. Large were they,
too, and loving—not merry, but still with a
smile playing at hide-and-seek in their depths,
ready to leap out at the faintest pretext. She
had dark eyebrows and long dark lashes,
white even teeth, and a round pretty chin, but
when all which could be said about her was
said, it was to her eyes everyone returned—
eyes that looked as a clear, deep river looks
when the sun is shining on it; eyes that were
indeed but windows through which the be-
holder might gaze straight down into a nature
strong, unselfish, truthful, and loving.

And yet she dwelt in that mean street, and
earned her living in that rough shed?

Yes; for we are rightly taught it is not
alone in kings' palaces God's elect are to be
found.

The smallest room or straitest of earth's
narrow places is wide enough and large
enough to contain a lovely spirit, a meek and
lowly heart.

I have said she sang, but it was only as one might play with the soft pedal so much down that the melody heard seemed scarce the echo of an air.

Yet it was a pretty old tune, with fine flowing words, fit to be flung to the winds on a hillside or lustily trolled in fields where the swarth, just cut, lay thick, and mowers sharpening their scythes paused to listen, and then took up the breezy chorus—true of and for all time—

> 'While the sun shines make hay,
> While the sun shines make hay,
> For ye cannot expect in December
> To gather the blossoms of May.'

Gently the knitting-needles clicked—a not unmusical accompaniment—then the girl's ball of worsted fell to the ground and she stooped to pick it up, ceasing her lay.

When she resumed her work she sang once more, but this time a mere commonplace ditty, which perhaps to her young heart seemed pleasingly sentimental.

> 'Only the old, old story
>   Whispered in mine ear ;
> Above was the summer glory,
>   Around the green wheat in ear.

'High in the cloudless heaven
    The lark sang loud and clear,
And we were alone together,
    I and my lover dear.

'Only as old a story
    As that which was whispered then '. . .

At which supreme point her voice trailed off into silence, and the rose-tints mantled in her cheeks, while she rose to greet a man who stepped across the threshold, and threaded his way through the baskets after the fashion of one accustomed to such exercise.

'So you are not holiday-making, Aileen,' he said.

'Indeed, no, Mr. Philip,' she answered in a soft, even voice, which held a charm in its tones. 'I went holiday-making once on Whit Monday, and I never want to go again. Won't you be pleased to sit down, sir?' and she indicated the bushel measure, which was the best apology for a chair the shed boasted.

'Thank you, I will find a seat for myself,' he answered, turning a basket bottom upwards. 'And you are all alone?'

'All alone, sir; they have gone every one of them to Hampton Court.'

'I am glad of that, for I want to speak to you.'

Unmistakably a gentleman, equally unmistakably the young fellow was not a lover—not Aileen's, at all events.

His manner to her, though perfectly friendly, more than friendly, indeed—familiar—was entirely innocent of even that harmless admiration a man of any rank may feel for a pretty girl, in whatsoever station it may have pleased God to place her.

Aileen's manner also, while equally unembarrassed, was that of an inferior towards a superior, of one who felt there lay so broad a gulf of caste between them that she could speak quite freely and naturally without the slightest fear of misconception.

That they knew each other very well, most intimately, indeed, was beyond doubt. Had she been his foster-sister, the sympathy and understanding between the curiously-assorted pair could not have seemed greater.

There was not the slightest awkwardness in their intercourse, no consciousness on either side, as in the most natural and simple way possible he asked :

'Are you not doing so well as you were, Aileen ?'

'I am doing a good trade, Mr. Philip,' the girl answered ; 'but I do not get a bit forward ; sometimes I think I never shall.'

'Why ?'

When two people understand each other few words suffice.

'It is this way, sir : whatever I make goes out as fast as I can get it. We might all be comfortable and happy as the day is long, but we are nothing of the sort. I am sure, the way things are, home is a misery.'

'So bad as that ?'

'Yes, as bad as that. I have been thinking about it all morning, and can see no light anywhere. Maybe it is wrong of me to be troubling you after your goodness in helping me to buy this good round, but——'

With a gesture the young man deprecated both the apology and the gratitude.

'I wish it had been in my power to do more for you,' he said.

'I know that, Mr. Philip, well, though you have done more for me than I can ever thank you enough for. The round is a good round,' she went on, reverting to the original question. 'The customers pay regularly, and never ask for credit unless they are out of work, and when they get in again bring their money as fast as they can, poor creatures! No; it is not that, and I should not so much mind it all being spent if there were ever an hour's peace or quiet. As much will be tossed away to-day as ought to keep the house for weeks, and it is the same always. Sometimes I feel I could walk out and never come back again. It is wrong, I dare say; I know it is wrong, but I can't help it.'

'I have always thought,' said the young man, 'you would be happier in a situation. If you were maid to some nice elderly lady——'

'I'd ask nothing better, Mr. Philip; but, then, no wages I could ask would serve to maintain them here. No; I must stop where I am as I am. Who would see to them if I went away? They would sell the business in a week, and live on the best till all the money was gone, and then end in the workhouse, likely as not. No, I must stay; I must——' and she stopped suddenly.

'Do you dislike the business, Aileen?'

'No, sir. Why should I dislike what buys us food and clothes and firing, and keeps a roof over us? What breaks my heart is that everything is so miserable when it might be so different. The boys are growing up rough and rude and wild, and what can I do for them? Mrs. Fermoy is vexed if I speak. She thinks they can do no wrong. There is not one of them but Jack of the least help. Peter would not be so bad if someone would show him a good example, but he is always copying Dick—smoking, swearing, drinking, and idling about the streets.'

'Nothing can be done for them, I suppose?'

'Nothing, sir; and I take shame to have said as much as I have, but there is no one except yourself that I can speak a word to, and my heart is so full and sore sometimes.'

'Poor girl!'

'Don't, Mr. Philip, don't, please, or you
will make me cry, and what would be the use
of that?'

'Not much, indeed. Tell me, is Mr.
Parkyn still with you?'

'He is, and I wish he was anywhere
else.'

'Has he gone to Hampton Court?'

'He, sir!—gone with our party, do you
mean? He is far too grand for that, and I
don't blame him, either. For all he lodges
with Mrs. Fermoy, Jack says he has seen
him on the top of a four-in-hand among a
lot of gentlemen. No; he went off early all
by himself in a gray dustcoat, with field-
glasses hung round him.'

'What is he?'

'A betting man, I think. I am told they
are one day up and another down, but whether
he is up or down, I am greatly afraid Mr.
Parkyn is not much good.'

'I saw your stepmother last week.'

'So she said, sir.'

'I was returning from Godalming, and at

Clapham Junction she chanced to get into the compartment with me. We had some conversation, and she seemed annoyed that you do not marry Mr. Parkyn.'

' I know she is—I know it well.'

' She said she thought it would be an excellent match for you.'

' I am sure she does.'

' And you, Aileen ?'

' What about me, Mr. Philip ?'

' My mother would have wished to know all about you once, I think.'

' And indeed, sir, your mother's son is welcome to know all about me now. Mr. Parkyn has never asked me to marry him, and never will.'

' But supposing he did ?'

' I can't suppose, Mr. Philip, that even a sham gentlemen like him could ever want to have anything to do with a girl like me.'

' Still, should the impossible happen ?'

' I'd say, '' Thank you kindly, sir, but no''—for, indeed, I could never take to him.'

' You are quite certain ?'

'I am quite certain.'

There ensued a pause, during which Aileen, with her pretty head bent down, tied and untied slip-knots in her worsted, while her friend Mr. Philip, taking out his pocket-book, searched among its contents till he found a scrap of newspaper.

'I think that ought to be seen to,' he said, handing her the cutting.

'What does it mean, sir?' she asked, after she had read it over.

'I have not the faintest idea,' he replied. 'Is there anyone who would be likely to leave him money?'

The girl shook her head. Then suddenly she seemed to see light.

'Perhaps General Galvaine is dead and has left him a legacy. He thought a lot of father.'

'General Galvaine is not dead. I saw his name in the paper only this morning.'

'Then I don't know what to think of this,' said Aileen, and she read slowly again, as if to impress its sense on her mind, the following advertisement:

'If Timothy Fermoy, who in the year 1860 kept a greengrocer's shop in Hornton Street, Kensington, will apply to Messrs. Desborne and Son, solicitors, Clock Lane, E.C., he will hear of something to his advantage.'

'But my poor father is dead.'

'Neither of us, Aileen, is likely to forget that. His daughter, however, is living.'

'Yes, sir.'

'And if this notice means that there would have been any money coming to him, it means most probably that there will be money coming to you. It may be, of course, that he is only wanted as having been witness to some deed, but in any case it would be right to call on these gentlemen and ascertain what the advertisement means. Shall I see them for you?'

'I could not think of putting you to such trouble, Mr. Philip,' answered the girl, in her soft, pleasant voice. 'I must go to market in the morning, and it is only a step across one of the bridges into the City.'

The young man looked thoughtfully at her, and then said 'Yes,' not at all as agreeing to the 'step across one of the bridges,' but merely as regarding the advisability of a personal visit to Messrs. Desborne and Son.

'Had you not better lock this cutting up?' he asked.

'If you could tell me the lock that would keep anything fast here, I would be for ever grateful to you, Mr. Philip.'

'Do you mean to say your places are opened?'

'Dick has got a second key to my box, and took five pounds out of it yesterday.'

'This is terrible, and I have not much that I can lend you.'

'I don't want you to lend me a penny, thank you, sir. There is an old woman, Mrs. Jeckels, in the market always lets me have what I need when I am short, only it is constantly like beginning over again.'

'Perhaps I had better write down Messrs. Desborne's address for you and tear up this advertisement.'

'I can put it away, thank you, where nobody will ever think of looking.'

'Where is that?'

'In my Bible, Mr. Philip.'

CHAPTER II.

EARLY the next morning Jack and Aileen started for the Borough Market. It is a long distance from Battersea, but they were well accustomed to the road—they and their smart little black donkey Parole, which both girl and boy fondly believed to be the best fed, best harnessed, best groomed, best housed, and fastest goer in all London.

As the donkey trotted through streets quiet and empty before the traffic of the day had begun, Jack talked about Hampton Court and what he saw there, and what a grand time they had, and of how they were obliged to walk up Kingston Hill because the horses were tired ; and how some of the excursionists must needs go on the river and nearly got upset—thousands of people, he said, went through the Palace; the rooms were so full they could not get near the pictures; he liked the grounds best, and the Maze: he thought he would walk down there by himself one Sunday, or he might—with a suggestive look—take the train from Clapham, it did not cost much.

'We will see what can be done, if you are a good boy,' answered Aileen. 'But, oh, Jack! how I am to make up that money Dick took I can't think. I was saving till the fruit came in, because you know how much we could have made last year about preserving time, and now every penny is gone, and I must borrow even for what we need this morning.'

Jack had no comfort to offer. In its way, the disaster was as great to this girl as the stoppage of a bank is to a depositor; five pounds —an immense capital—now cast to the four winds of heaven by Dick the irreclaimable.

'He won't come back this while,' observed the boy; but even this certainty failed to prove a solace to Aileen.

If not at home he would be probably in some much worse place.

'Tom says he'll give him a good hiding,' went on the boy; but still Aileen kept silence. She knew that medicine ought to have been administered many a year before, and felt doubtful as to the effect of it or any other domestic drug likely to be given, especially by Tom, who was as poor a moral doctor as any patient could desire to be under.

'Have you no money at all left, Ally?' asked Jack, when the long pause had become monotonous.

'Only a few shillings,' she answered. 'I gave all I had except that five pounds to your mother.'

'Couldn't you have got some from Mr. Parkyn?'

'No,' answered Aileen, so shortly that the lad cast about for some other subject of conversation.

There are times when if one thing goes wrong some other thing is sure to follow suit. Joy is sufficient to itself, but sorrow loves company, and it was for this reason probably that when Aileen made her way to Mrs. Jeckels' stand she found a total stranger in possession, who explained that the old lady had been taken bad on Sunday; that he was her nephew, and that his wife would stay in London 'for a bit' to look after his aunt.

'What is the matter?' asked the girl.

'The doctor didn't rightly say, but my own notion is that it's a break-up. She has been an uncommon active woman, but no woman can go on for ever. It is what we must all come to.'

With the sun shining on the tower of St. Mary Overie, which rose in its stately proportions so high above where they stood, and the graves of hundreds long dead close beside them, this general statement was not one easily controverted. Aileen, at all events, made no effort to prove Mrs. Jeckels' nephew in error.

She only spoke a few words of sympathy and turned away, wondering what she had better do under such unexpected circumstances.

The matter was pressing ; she could not go back empty unless she wanted to risk her trade ; she must try to get credit—a thing she had never done before, because credit is not a system of business which finds favour in the Borough Market.

There was only one man in it she knew sufficiently well to ask for even a few days' grace, and she did not feel at all certain that he would grant such a boon. However, the position had to be faced, and as there was no use in delaying her petition, Aileen walked round the flagged enclosure till she reached Mr. Plashet's stand.

Mr. Plashet was the antipodes of Mrs. Jeckels, over the whole of whose ample person ' country ' was writ large, and whose tongue betrayed her whenever she opened her mouth.

Mr. Plashet, on the contrary, stood a Londoner, and gloried in the fact. To him there seemed no place like it, and no place within the bills of mortality or out of that boundary so charming as Southwark, and, finally, no place in Southwark so altogether

desirable as the Borough Market and its
environs.

He was a very shrewd man of business,
but he did not therefore consider little vices
to be despised.   On the contrary, he thought
many of them were to be preferred to virtues.
There was a bar near at hand he much
affected, where 'Irish' of a peculiarly soft
and mellow flavour could be obtained, as
well as a glass of port wine 'no alderman
need have refused.'

Likewise, there was a certain bar parlour
where a few friends often met in order to
pass a convivial evening, in which he sang
a good song with the best.   Further, his
admirers, who were numerous, affirmed that
he was an excellent judge of a play, that he
knew who could be depended on to win the
next billiard contest, that he was acquainted
with those who gave him sure tips concerning
equine favourites, and had certain information about noted pugilists and the man who
would walk away with Doggett's coat and
badge.

In a word, he was a paragon of learning,

which, perhaps, accounted for the fact that in general company his manners left something to be desired. ' Till you understood him,' said his friends, ' anyone might think him a little short '—a mark of great intellect, doubtless, but one which had the disadvantage of occasionally causing him to be considered surly.

In person he was tall, thin, and haggard-looking, with straight light hair and sallow complexion, and a general effect as if he had for a long time been burning his candle at both ends, which possibly was the fact.

On that Whit Tuesday morning he had a particularly seedy appearance, while he talked to three other men who looked even more washed - out than himself, notwithstanding their having evidently striven quite lately to ' fix ' such colour as nature had vouchsafed them at the bar afore honourably mentioned.

One of these gentlemen wore a tall hat, white, with a mourning band round it, that seemed to have been in the wars, which he took off at intervals, surveyed, and then stuck jauntily on his head again with a sigh and a smile, inspired probably by memories of the preceding evening's drive Londonward in company with a merry party.

When Aileen paused by Mr. Plashet's stand, that autocrat acknowledged her shy 'Good-morning, sir,' with a nod that could not be considered promising.

She did not mind this very much, however, because she knew the good man's ways, but the strangers were a trial, and as she named the goods required, and added : 'I'll bring what they come to next time, if you please,' her voice shook a little.

Good or bad, Mr. Plashet took no notice of her words. He refrained equally from saying ' That will do ' or ' That will not do,' ' You can have what you want ' or ' You cannot,' but took a short lounge into his crowded store with that lazy, swinging gait which passed among his admirers as the height of swelldom.

' Look alive, Jake,' he said to a burly individual who was leaning against some sacks of potatoes piled one on the top of another that formed an appropriate background to the picture ; but what Jake was to look alive

about Mr. Plashet did not condescend to explain.   He only made a languid dive beneath
his standing desk, and came up with a long
thin book, which he opened and then began
to write.

Aileen waited. This was an experience
quite out of her customary routine, yet she
did not despair. No one knew better than
she how odd the salesman could be, and she
did not intend to meet a denial half-way.

'You went pleasuring yesterday, I suppose?'
said Mr. Plashet at last, pausing in his occu-
pation to make the remark.

'No, sir; but my money did,' answered
Aileen. The reply was simple enough, but
the effect it produced was great.

All the men, except Mr. Plashet, who
smiled languidly, burst out laughing, the
white-hatted individual placing his hands on
his knees, and bending himself almost double
in his mirth.

'Blest if that ain't a good one!' he exclaimed. 'Hanged if I know when I've
heard a better bit! So your money took
Scot's leave, did it, my dear?'

' Yes, it did,' Aileen answered shortly.

' Well, well, don't break your heart about it ; there is more in the Bank of England. Care killed a cat, though certainly history does not say when. Really you are a very pretty young woman. What's your particular, darling ?'

' I don't drink,' was the reply.

' It's time you began, then ; you'll never learn younger.'

' I never intend to learn at all,' retorted Aileen.

' Come, come, that's all very nice, but we know what it means.'

' Mind what you are about, Johnston,' interrupted Mr. Plashet at this supreme moment.

' Eh ! Did you speak ?' said Mr. Johnston, with affected surprise.

' I did. I told you to mind what you are about. If you don't know a respectable girl when you see her, it is time you were taught.'

' And who could teach me ?' asked Mr. Johnston.

' I could, and I will,' replied Mr. Plashet.

'Oh yes, we know all about you,' returned Mr. Johnston, at which phrase, regarded—as for some inscrutable reason it is by a certain class—as the very essence of wit, the three visitors had another explosion of mirth which effectually dispersed the gathering storm.

'No offence meant, miss; no offence taken, I hope,' said the gentleman in the white hat, removing his head-gear and making an elaborate bow as he spoke.

'No offence taken,' answered Aileen, with frank civility. 'May I tell Jack to bring the baskets round, Mr. Plashet?' she added, determined to bring matters to a point.

'Jake can take some of them to the cart for you,' answered the arbiter of her destiny for that hour.

'Perish the thought!' cried Mr. Johnston. 'Here, Hime and Simmonds, bear a hand!' And before anyone could say a word the three gay spirits were racing over the pavement with two bushel measures, Mr. Hime and Mr. Johnston carrying one, and Mr. Johnston and Mr. Simmonds the other, the white-hatted gentleman thus bearing a double burden, perhaps by way of expiation.

'Clear the course, clear the course!' he shouted, as they rushed excitedly on. 'Keep out of the way, or you'll get run over,' and thus they reached the street, Mr. Plashet shouting after them, 'Stole away! stole away!' followed by about a score of small lads and a couple of indignant porters, who saw in anticipation their dues disappearing, and pursued with the intention of rescuing them by fair means or foul.

Aileen had stopped but to speak a word of grateful thanks to Mr. Plashet, and followed close on the heels of her cavaliers.

Light of foot, and unencumbered, she came up with them while they were crying aloud as with one voice, 'Jack, Jack, Jack, Jack! Where the deuce are you, Jack? Who the deuce is Jack?'

'That is Jack, on the other side with the donkey-cart,' explained the donkey-cart's owner.

'Have at him, then!' exclaimed Mr. Johnston, and at this word of command the three warriors charged the crossing, as they had charged the market, bearing down all before them, and still pursued by the boys and the porters.

'Jack,' said Aileen, ' run with the baskets and sacks to Mr. Plashet—fast, now, and I will look after the donkey.'

'Not while your humble servant is here to command,' observed Mr. Johnston, striking an attitude. 'Will you oblige me,' he added, addressing his following, ' by leaving the coast clear? If you must admire, let it be from a suitable distance. Money, is it? Oh, with pleasure; but really I am afraid I have nothing less than a five-pound note. Can you oblige me with change? No? Then proceed to Mr. Plashet——'

What he meant to say concerning Mr. Plashet, however, can only be conjectured, for at a sign from Aileen the porters had already departed.

'I fear you tipped those miscreants,' said Mr. Johnston, 'instead of leaving me to deal with them. Well, policeman, and what do you think of it all?'

The policeman thus addressed did not answer. He only looked benignly over his stock at the three friends, Aileen and the donkey, and then said to the boys in a tone of authority, and with a side movement of his head :

'Come you, be off now !'

'Yes ; to your play or to your school,' supplemented Mr. Johnston, 'though I believe it is that terrible time called vacation. The future hopes of England,' he added, waving his hands towards the young imps ; ' raw material.'

'Mighty raw,' remarked his friend, Mr. Hime.

'They are what you were,' replied Mr. Johnston severely.

'Very like an epitaph that, isn't it ?' was Mr. Hime's retort.

And so the foolish babble flew like chaff before the wind ; while Aileen, after vainly essaying to assume control of Parole, stood a little apart, awaiting the arrival of the rest of her goods.

They came erelong, and were built so

scientifically on the cart that the donkey had not, as Jack observed, ' an ounce weight on his back,' to remedy which defect, as doubtless he considered it, Mr. Johnston, after resigning Parole's head to the boy, advanced towards Aileen, and inquired if he might have the honour of handing her to her carriage.

' We shall walk,' said the girl.

' Walk !' repeated Mr. Johnston. ' Angels and ministers of grace, where is the fairy godmother ? where is the chariot ? where the fairy steeds ? where the gorgeous apparelled menials ? where the glass slippers ? where, above all, the prince ?'

' That don't much signify, as he ain't here,' observed his friend Mr. Simmonds—candid, as is the manner of friends.

' We will wish you good-morning, sir,' remarked Aileen, with a glance which took in Messrs. Hime and Simmonds as well as Mr. Johnston. ' We have a long step to go, and the sooner we start the better.'

' It always comes to this,' observed Mr. Johnston; ' as someone has correctly observed,

" we meet to part, like ships on the great sea "
—a fine idea !   Good-day, then, pretty brown
eyes ; may you sell your roots and herbs to
advantage, and keep a sunny place in thy
memory, dearest, for yours to command,
T. Johnston !—Now, gentlemen, right about
face ;' and they ran back as they had come,
only this time hand in hand, to the admiration of all beholders.

The policeman looked after them, and then
relaxed into a smile.

'Their tea was made too strong this morning,' he observed enigmatically.

'They meant no harm,' returned Aileen,
who from her association with Messrs. Jack,
Peter, and Dick perfectly understood dark
sayings as applied to common matters.

'I thought I might as well wait to see.'

'I saw you did,' said Aileen ; ' thank you ;'
and she emphasized her gratitude with that
most useful and, in certain circles, familiar
form of currency, twopence.

The girl and boy walked on in perfect
silence till Southwark Bridge Road was
crossed, Parole stepping out as though he

had pledged his word to put his very best foot
foremost.

From time to time Jack glanced at his
companion's face, but there was nothing to be
gathered from its expression. He had never
before seen her in a precisely similar mood,
and, unable to reconcile the amount of goods
she had procured with such unusual preoccu-
pation, he bethought him of a cause which
might account for what he mentally called
her dumps.

' Did those toffs vex you, Ally ?' he asked.

She raised her head and looked at him in
surprise.

' No,' she replied. ' What made you think
of such a thing ?'

' You are so deedy, and they were such
queer chaps.'

' They won't be so queer to-morrow, most
likely. Yesterday isn't long gone, and they
are not quite sober yet, and still full of their
fun.'

' Is that all ?'

' That is all. They were in Mr. Plashet's
when I got there, and began chaffing, and

then nothing would serve them but to play at being porters.'

'I see,' said Jack, who did not see in the least, and did not believe, either, having the usual suspiciousness of his sex when his own female belongings were in question. 'And they did not vex you ?' with lingering incredulity.

'They did not ; but I was vexed at having to go to Mr. Plashet.'

'Why, he always serves you well.'

'He does, but I had to ask him for credit.'

'How was that ?   Would Mrs. Jeckels not lend you enough ?'

'Mrs. Jeckels was not in the market.   She is ill.'

Jack whistled.

'It is lucky you got credit, anyhow,' he remarked.

'It is, but I'll have to take good care of all the money we can scrape together to pay Mr. Plashet, and have something for next market-day.   As I told you coming down, I must go into the City, and may not get back home before you have finished your first round. Promise me you'll give nobody even sixpence, no matter what it is wanted for.'

'Nobody 'll get a farden out of me,' said Jack valiantly. 'I suppose you mean I'm not to let mother have anything?'

'I mean that you are to keep whatever you take till I get home. It's not yours to give, and it is not mine either, for that matter. It is Mr. Plashet's, so do what I tell you, like a dear lad.'

'All right,' he answered. 'I say, Ally, lend me your bag to put the takings in.'

She handed him a little chamois bag, such as small tradesmen who go often to the bank are in the habit of carrying. It contained but a few pence, out of which she kept three for travelling expenses.

'Is that all there is left?' queried the boy.

'That is all,' she answered, and they walked on in silence, both sometimes in the horseway, Aileen occasionally on the curb, but always close together, and stepping out briskly to keep pace with Parole, who after two days'

rest was fresh as a daisy, and, indeed, had for
very playfulness kicked and shown his teeth
when Mr. Johnston essayed to show how well
he understood donkey weaknesses—by pulling
his ears.

They did not talk much after this. The
traffic of the day had begun, and it is not easy
to carry on a conversation when guiding a
donkey-cart between vans and omnibuses, cabs
and drags and private traps. Thus it happened that, save for an occasional remark, they
traversed in silence Southwark, Holland, and
Stamford Streets, York Road, crossed Westminster Bridge Road, passed the south side of
St. Thomas's Hospital, skirted the gardens of
Lambeth Palace, and finally reached that point
where in olden times the Horseferry boats
touched the Surrey side.

There, just opposite the ancient gateway and
St. Mary's Church, Aileen stopped and said :

'I'll take the boat from here, Jack. You
won't forget what I told you ?'

'No fear,' returned the boy.

'And you may just as well ride home.
Your weight won't make any difference.'

'No, he'll never feel it,' which was perhaps
more than Parole would have said; nevertheless, the arrangement was satisfactorily carried
out, and when Aileen looked back before going
down the steps she saw Jack snugly ensconced
among the baskets, and the donkey start
gallantly off at a round trot for Battersea.

CHAPTER III.

A STEAMER was leaving Vauxhall Pier as
Aileen put her penny through the pigeon-hole
at Lambeth pay-office and received in return
a ticket available at any of the six landing-
stages which end with that of the Old Swan.

It is cheap travelling and pleasant when the
boats are not over-crowded. Of a winter's
morning, with only two or three passengers
on board and freedom to stand close by the
funnel, it is as nice a way of getting into the
City as anyone need desire. How well London
looks from the river! With what an easy,
gliding movement the Archbishop's Palace is
left behind, and the great hospital and the
Houses of Parliament passed, then under
Westminster Bridge, and on beside the Vic-

toria Embankment, till Somerset House is
reached, and the dome of St. Paul's looms
larger and nearer every second. A wonderful
run for a penny, with a fresh wind blowing off
the Thames, and picturesque barges going up
with the tide, and the great warehouses below
Blackfriars taking in or sending off cargoes of
goods. with lighters lying at anchor all along
Bankside, where the gardens of Winchester
House used to slope to the river, and the sun
shining on scores of City churches and gilding
their fanes anew !

Seated on one of the centre benches in the
forepart of the steamboat, whither she had
modestly taken up her quarters, careful not to
intrude her humble personality upon people
better dressed and apparently more prosperous,
Aileen Fermoy looked at the spires and wondered, as well she might, how many a person
could count between Blackfriars and Old Swan
Pier.

She knew nothing of the City history, or
else what a tale she might have recited to
herself as the boat swept down the river, till
at last it slackened speed and stopped hard by

the spot where Osborne took that adventurous
leap to save a child's life, which, in our
degenerate times, one or two others have
repeated for money.

Familiar as the Borough Market was to her,
she had never even heard the 'true history
(probably false) of the life and sudden death
of old John Overs, the rich ferryman of
London, showing how he lost his life by his
own covetousness. And of his daughter Mary,
who caused the church of St. Mary Overie,
Southwark, to be built, and of the building of
London Bridge.'

Nor in her stock of old ballads had the
nurse's song a place :

> ' London Bridge is broken down,
>   Dance over, my Lady Lea ;
> London Bridge is broken down,
>   With a gay lady '—

song dear to the hearts of children, who joined
in the chorus with their young voices and kept
time to its music with their merry, restless feet
centuries ago.

She did not know there had ever been houses
on the bridge, or so-called traitors' heads set on

high there, or that, landing at the Old Swan, close to where she herself stepped from the steamboat, Eleanor, Duchess of Gloucester, began one of her public penances for the sin of witchcraft. Over and over again she had stood under the shadow of St. Mary Overie and yet never entered the Lady's Chapel. There had been no one to tell her of the Tabard Inn, and show her in fancy the Canterbury Pilgrims who lodged there and will haunt the place for ever, though no stone of the building remains to reward curious sight-seekers, and modern London like a mighty ocean sweeps over those ancient landmarks, the memory of which it, nevertheless, fails to obliterate. No —though the girl's was a nature to have been fascinated by the story of olden times, all the traditions of the past were as a sealed book to her.

She was too young to remember even that now comparatively old London middle-aged people love with a tender sadness to recall. Born before any of the great works completed during the last twenty-five years were begun, she had, nevertheless, no memory of a time

when Broad Street Station, the Metropolitan
Railway, the Thames Embankment, Queen
Victoria Street, giant hotels, board schools,
Civil Service stores, were not—of a time, in
fact, as one of the present generation might
naturally suggest, when nothing was.

How did people get on a quarter of a
century ago without all the modern improve-
ments they are at present blessed with?

Well, much as they get on now. They ate,
they drank, they married and were given in
marriage, they struggled through life's little
day more or less successfully; they suffered,
they grew aged, they laughed, they wept, they
cheated, they were cheated, they did brave
deeds, they were guilty of villainy, they fell
sick and recovered, or they fell sick and died,
and passed into the Silent Land precisely as
folks do to this hour.

The centuries come and the centuries go
while the main facts of existence change not at
all. The fashions of this world may vary, but
the human nature which sets or follows those
fashions does not alter, as many worthy indi-
viduals imagine.

Aileen was a Londoner bred and born, and not one of the sights in the city she walked through looked strange to her, yet she felt lonely, because the streets she paced were not those habit had made familiar.

It was another phase of Metropolitan life from any she was well acquainted with which presented itself. In Battersea, for example, she knew many persons both by sight and to speak to, and even in the thoroughfares leading to the Borough Market she often met chance acquaintances who exchanged greetings with her.

When she got into Swan Lane all this was changed, and, though not shy, she began to feel timid about her visit to Messrs. Desborne's office.

The day had not begun well for her. There are days in which everything seems to go wrong, and for Aileen so far that promised to be one of them.

She had risen with a headache, consequent upon having been obliged to sit up late the night before. Mrs. Jeckels' illness troubled her, for the poor old lady had often proved a friend in need; the experience with Mr. Plashet's merry gentlemen could not be regarded by a quiet modest girl as exactly agreeable; and, worse than all, she did not see her way about matters at home.

While it lasted, the quick run down the river —the keen air—the bright sunshine—the succession of changing objects—the very landing of some passengers and taking on of others, had roused and done her good, but once more on terra firma, the former dejection resumed its sway.

Out of spirits herself, the 'day after the fair' look of those she met struck her as very depressing also. On some mornings—and, for that matter, on some evenings too—only the men and women who know nothing they are wanted to know chance to be abroad.

On that morning no one had even so much as heard of Cloak Lane, but many were quite certain it was Cross Lane, or Finch Lane, or Petticoat Lane, or Cloth Fair, Aileen was searching for.

The persons she asked belonged to that curious type who, if an inquirer wishes to be

put in the right way for Pudding Lane, at once
assume Pie Corner must be meant, and it was
more by accident than owing to any wit or
wisdom on the part of those who vouchsafed
information that she did not find herself in
Houndsditch, or threading the mazes of Bartholomew Close, Little Britain, and Long Lane,
but was only merrily tossed like a shuttlecock
from Cannon to Thames Street, from Thames
Street to Fenchurch Street, and thence back to
Cannon Street, where the scent of course lay
warm. Still, she was not aware of that, and
for some time pursued her inquiries without
getting much nearer her object.

She asked a shopboy, who did not think
there was such a place. She asked a cabman,
who replied he did not know much about the
City. She asked a poorly-dressed woman,
who said, 'I am sorry I can't tell you.' She
asked a mechanic, and he answered, 'I am a
stranger myself.' Then she stopped a work-
girl, who made the consolatory observation,
'I am sure it is not in the City. You had
better try the other side of the water.' She
could not see a policeman, and though she ran

after a letter-carrier, she only nearly reached that functionary in time to watch him ascending a steep flight of stairs, up which she did not like to follow.

She was wandering in the direction of Cheapside, and would possibly have taken a turn round the Mansion House, the Royal Exchange, and the Bank of England, had she not happened to espy a telegraph messenger.

' If you please,' she cried, ' will you tell me where to find Cloak Lane ?' as if Cloak Lane had been carelessly mislaid somewhere.

' Why, you are coming away from it ! Cross Cannon Street ; first turn to the left, as you go to Southwark Bridge. You can't miss it ;' and the lad, who had paused in his haste to answer, ran off, leaving Aileen to think what a civil, well-spoken little chap he was, to wonder how boys fell into such berths, and to wish her brothers—so-called—had a chance of getting into any employment of the sort.

Following his directions, in less than a minute she found the place she had been in search of, and which she must have passed close to over and over again.

Walking slowly down one side of the lane and then crossing to the other and repeating her performance, she still failed to see the name she was in search of, and had to seek information from a porter who was in charge of a truck opposite one of the houses.

For answer he pointed to a door close at hand, and said, 'Go in there.'

Aileen did as she was directed, and when she entered was rewarded by seeing 'Clerks' Office' painted so that they who ran might read.

Taking her courage in her hand, she knocked on the panel. There was no answer, so she knocked again louder.

'Come in,' called out a sharp voice, and Aileen, opening the door, crossed the threshold.

Near the window a man sat at a high desk writing. Behind a short counter, doing nothing, stood a young fellow, who looked at the girl as she walked forward with the expression of a person who felt convinced she had strayed in by mistake.

A pen was stuck jauntily behind his right

ear, and he arrested attention not merely by reason of the plainness of his face, but also because of the perfect self-satisfaction which clothed him as with a garment.

Aileen had seen that morning some hundreds of smart, good-looking, well-set-up young clerks, but not one of them attracted or remained in her memory as did this ugly piece of lively impudence, who, putting the palms of both hands flat on the counter, bent over it with a sort of 'What for you, miss?' expression beaming in his face, which was eminently disconcerting.

'Is Mr. Desborne in?' asked the girl, thus settling the question as to whether she had wandered there by chance in the negative.

'I regret to say he is not,' answered the clerk, who at once saw an opportunity which he did not mean to lose.

In truth, poor Aileen looked as little like a possible client to such a firm as can well be imagined.

Her black straw bonnet, if not worn quite at the altitude affected by peripatetic green-

grocers of her own sex, was perched sufficiently high on her head to afford some
protection from the sun.

'It was cocked up like a haymaker's,'
explained Mr. Tripsdale subsequently, 'and
she had a great white linen apron over a
clean print gown, and a jacket that had
seen hard service on the top of that. 'Pon
my honour I made sure she had come about
some Old Bailey case—assault, or passing
bad coin, or burglary. You might have
knocked me over with a feather when I
heard her errand.'

But Aileen did not tell him her errand
then, or ever. Knowledge came to Mr.
Tripsdale otherwise. When she found Mr.
Desborne was not in, she asked :

'Can I see his son ?'

'Well, the fact is,' answered Mr. Tripsdale, leaning more and more over the counter,
and speaking in a private and confidential
tone, 'that we have no son here. Mr.
Edward Desborne was once the son when he
had a father, but he has no father now, and
he would be the father if he had a son,

which he has not.   I trust I make my meaning clear ?'

'You mean, I suppose, there is no one I
can speak to about the matter that brought
me into the City ?' said Aileen.

'Unless I can be of service,' suggested
Mr. Tripsdale, with a smile which added
quite a weird attraction to his face.

'What is the best time to see Mr. Desborne ?' asked the girl, passing by this
generous offer as unworthy of notice.

For answer Mr. Tripsdale looked at the
clock which ticked above the chimney-piece,
then he took out a silver watch and con-
sulted it, before he said :

'Really, as a rule, I do not think you
could better this hour.   Mr. Desborne generally reaches the office at an early period of
the day, but these holiday times make us
all a little unpunctual. If you were to tell
me the nature of your business I might be
able to save you a journey.'

'Thank you ; but I want to see Mr.
Desborne.'

'I assure you Mr. Desborne is not always

to be seen. He is often engaged in writing, for instance, or has clients with him, and could not perhaps make leisure to see you when you called, happy though he would be to do so, I have no doubt, if it were possible. Really, you had better indicate the matter which is engaging your attention, or at least leave your name and address.'

'If Mr. Desborne was in he would see me, I think,' said Aileen, not without dignity, though there were tears in her eyes and her cheeks were unusually red. 'I am often near here, so I will take my chance and call some other day. Good-morning;' and she was turning to go, when the man who had been writing got down off his stool, caught Mr. Tripsdale by the arm, and muttering, 'Don't be such an ass!' jerked him from the counter.

'Mr. Desborne is rather uncertain,' he went on, addressing the girl, 'and you might call here many times and not find him unless you had an appointment. Is there nothing I can attend to for you? Perhaps I could advise you to whom to apply if you are in any difficulty.'

'You are very kind—but I am not in any difficulty, thank you. It is Mr. Desborne I want to see, and I must just call till I do see him. Good-day, sir;' and this time she really left the office, when Mr. Tripsdale walked across the floor on tiptoe, the better to indicate unbounded astonishment, which proceeding drew from the elder clerk an expression of belief that he was a confounded fool.

'Did you ever, ever,' hummed Mr. Tripsdale, 'did you ever, ever, did you ever see a wha-ha-a-al, did you ever, ever——'

'Stop that row, can't you!' interrupted the other. 'I have seen you, and that's enough,' which was a singularly inappropriate retort, since Mr. Tripsdale was in every respect unlike a whale of any known species.

Meanwhile Aileen, after pausing on the step, proceeded in the direction of Dowgate Hill. At that moment a gentleman walking on the opposite side of the way left the curb and crossed the lane, the pleasantest-looking gentleman, Aileen thought, she had ever seen—so pleasant-looking, in fact, that she turned her head and stared after him, a fault of which no Lady Clara Vere de Vere would, of course, have been guilty—a fault, indeed, into which this poor girl was not in the habit of falling ; but now, when she did fall into it, she saw that on the threshold she had just left the gentleman was standing looking after her with an amused and genial sort of curiosity.

Instantly it flashed through Aileen's mind that this pleasant gentleman was the one she sought, and without stopping to think, she turned back, and asked on the spur of the moment :

' Oh, please, sir, are you Mr. Desborne ?'

' My name is Desborne,' he said. ' Can I do anything for you ?'

' I did want to see you, sir—about this,' and she gave him the newspaper cutting, at which he glanced in evident surprise.

' And what have you to do with Timothy Fermoy ?' he inquired.

' He was my father, sir.'

' Was ?   Is he dead, then ?'

' Yes, sir; he died four years ago the tenth of last March.'

' You had better come in,' said Mr. Desborne, and he held first the outer door, then the door of the clerks' office, and finally the door leading into his own private room, open for her to pass through.

' Here's a go !' remarked Mr. Tripsdale, the moment principal and client had disappeared.

' I hope this will be a warning to you,' said his senior, with a severity which was assumed to conceal his own astonishment.

CHAPTER IV.

PROBABLY there was not in the city of London a pleasanter man to talk to than Mr. Edward Desborne.

He was not merely pleasant to talk to, but pleasant in every relation of life. He overflowed with kindness. He never felt so happy as when conferring a favour, or subscribing to a charity, or helping some widow in her need, or assisting a hard-worked father to keep his legs or get on them again.

Many men obtain a character for goodness on insufficient grounds, but Edward Desborne deserved every word of praise which was spoken concerning him, and many that were never uttered.

For his kindness was as warm as the sun,

as gracious as summer rain, and his manners
were of that delightful sort which make those
who come under their influence better and
more charitable.

There was in his nature no sham or pretence
of any description. Where others said, ' Poor
fellow !' or ' How sad !' and immediately
forgot the sadness and the poor fellow, Mr.
Desborne's first speech would be, ' What can
we do for him ?' thus crediting friends and
neighbours with his own generous desires,
and so wrapping the whole human family in
his own philanthropic mantle.

He had been popular all his life—at school,
at college, in the office where he served his
time, and now, when over forty, he was
popular in the City, in society, and at his club.

The one place where, perhaps, he stood on
a lower platform was his home, but the
cause chanced to be that he had married a
lady of higher rank than his own, who did not
love him quite so much as he loved her. In
fact, she did not love him at all, for the sufficient reason that she could not love anyone
greatly except herself.

Mr. Desborne, however, simply adored his wife. To him she seemed the truest lady, the noblest woman earth ever beheld. In his eyes she could do nothing but what was right; her wishes always appeared reasonable, the only sorrow he ever felt being that anything he could offer should prove so utterly unworthy her acceptance.

His affection would have exhausted the mines of Golconda, and lavished all the gold King Solomon gathered together. He deemed himself quite unfit to possess such a treasure. It was a delight to him even to see her cross a room, to hear her footfall on the stairs, to listen to her voice—ay, even to imagine her shadow touched him as she passed !

Never was a woman loved with a devotion so entire, so unselfish ; and the world, looking kindly on, thought what a perfect creature she must be to inspire such worship.

Edward Desborne, in addition to being a model husband, was very good to look at. Though forty, his blue eyes had still a bright, boyish expression, which proved infinitely charming. Tall, fair, light-haired, clean-shaven, Aileen Fermoy made no mistake when she decided he was the very pleasantest gentleman her eyes had ever beheld. He was pleasant to everyone—from a crossing-sweeper to the best client his firm could boast. To all women he was chivalrous, and though, in Aileen's case, it might be supposed his politeness proceeded from interested motives, it is but fair to say he would have been equally courteous to the humblest house-wife who on Saturday night spent her husband's hardly-earned wages to the best advantage in High Street, Hoxton.

After they had entered his private office he placed a chair for Timothy Fermoy's daughter, and when, after a moment's hesitation, the girl sat down, he drew one forward for himself, saying at the same time:

'Now let me hear all about it.'

To Aileen's comprehension it seemed that it was she who had come to hear 'all about' whatever there was to tell, so she answered in her own pretty modest way:

'Indeed, sir, I know nothing.'

He smiled, and she could not help smiling

in return. ' Really a pretty girl,' he thought ;
' a nice, frank, pretty girl ! What a pity—
what a thousand pities !' which mental remark
had no connection with her looks, bad or good.

' How did you happen to see this advertisement ?' he asked.

' A gentleman showed it to me yesterday,
and said it ought to be attended to.'

' Quite so '—an observation which might
have meant much or little. ' You will not
mind answering a few questions ?'

' Oh no, sir.'

Mr. Desborne stretched out his hand to
touch the bell, but on second thoughts drew
it back again, and, taking a sheet of paper,
lifted a pencil, looked at it, and then observed :

' And so you are the daughter of Timothy
Fermoy ?'

' Yes, sir ; my mother never had another
child.'

' Do you know where he was born ?'

' He was born and bred in Clontarf, not far
out of Dublin, but his father came from
King's County.'

' Oh ! wbat was his father ?'

' Coachman, sir, to Admiral Cecil.'

' Yes ; just tell me anything that occurs to you about your parents, and I can ask you such questions as occur to me afterwards.'

It was not difficult for Aileen to talk about herself and her belongings. In that rank of life egotism is even more natural than in a higher, and therefore, after the first awkwardness of speaking freely to a stranger, and that stranger a gentleman, she proceeded without hesitation to explain how her father when a lad went as boy under the butler at Admiral Cecil's establishment, and how, when he knew his business thoroughly, General Galvaine took him for his own butler. ' My mother was lady's-maid to Mrs. Galvaine,' the girl added, ' and so they became acquainted.'

' I understand.'

' When they had saved enough money they made up their minds to get married and start a greengrocer's shop in Kensington, where they did well till my mother died.'

' Yes, and then ?'

' My father's health broke, and he thought

he would make a shift, so he sold his business, and bought another in Kennington Park
Road.'

'That is rather odd,' said Mr. Desborne,
looking thoughtfully down on the paper, which
he tapped with his pencil; then, as an idea
struck him, he asked, 'Did he trade in his own
name?'

'No, sir; he took the shop off a man called
Fidgeley, and never changed the name above
the door. It was more convenient. There
were bill-heads and all.'

'I see; did he die there?'

'He died in Guy's Hospital.'

'Badly off?'

'Not to say badly off, sir; only the doctors
thought he'd have better care there, and that
he might get strong again. But his heart was
broken. He never rightly held up his head
after my mother's death.'

'Ah! very sad; and where have you been
living since?'

'With Mrs. Fermoy.'

'Who is she — what relation to you, I
mean?'

'She's my father's widow, sir. Before he died he married her, for he thought it would be hard for me to be left alone in the world if anything happened to him, and indeed she is a good-natured woman.'

'You don't call her mother?'

'No, sir.'

'Do you not agree?'

'We agree well enough,' answered Aileen, for the first time with a certain constraint, 'but I don't hold with second marriages myself.'

'Clearly a young person possessed of decided opinions,' thought Mr. Desborne.

'What do you do for a living? Are you tolerably comfortable?'

'We can't complain, sir. There was plenty of furniture, and Mrs. Fermoy lets off enough to pay the rent, and something more. Then the gentleman that showed me your advertisement lent me as much money as bought a round.'

'What is a round?' asked Mr. Desborne.

'You may have a round of anything, sir— fish or firewood or cat's-meat, or mending kettles and such-like, or vegetables—mine is vegetables—and fruit,' she added as an after-thought, ' when it comes in.'

' But how do you manage ? I don't understand,' he said.

' I go round, sir. In my father's time of course we were in a better way, and he only called on his customers for orders and de-livered the goods ; but people like us go round to sell what we can, not to gentry, but to the working men's wives and that sort.'

' It must be a very hard life.'

' Not so hard as anyone might think. We have to be out in all weathers, of course, but we don't get wet through very often. The worst of it is going to market so early in the winter mornings ; but, indeed, sir, I'm very thankful to be able to earn as much as I do. Besides, Jack is a good lad,' she added, with an evident desire to do full justice to that young gentleman's abilities—' he can hallo so loud.'

' But why does he hallo ?' asked Mr. Des-borne, mystified, though interested.

' To let people know we are in the street, sir, and what we have in the cart with us.'

' Oh, I comprehend,' said Mr. Desborne, to whom there recurred the memory of ear-splitting yells which he had heard when passing through a certain lane in the neigh-bourhood of Holborn. ' Is it necessary to shout so loudly ?'

' Yes, sir ; we should do no trade if some-body did not hallo. When I began I had to hire a lad, but he was not worth half as much as Jack. Shouting that way spoils a boy's voice, though, completely—makes it hoarse and rough.'

' Spoils it for singing, I suppose you mean.'

' Yes, or for talking. Perhaps, sir, you have never spoken to a coster ; but if you had, you could not help noticing the sort of voice most of them have. You would think they had a bad cold. That comes from crying out what they have to sell.'

' Does it indeed ? Poor fellows !'

' I am often sorry for them myself,' said Aileen, touched by a sympathetic tone in

Mr. Desborne's voice; 'many of them are such industrious, civil chaps.'

'I have no doubt of it; but Jack isn't a costermonger, is he?'

'No, sir; he is Mrs. Fermoy's son.'

'And consequently your brother.'

'In a sort of a way, sir.'

Mr. Desborne glanced back over the few notes he had made, which had seemed to Aileen written by magic, till he came to this, 'The only child my mother ever had.' Then he turned to Aileen, and said:

'Your father having married a second time, your stepmother's sons must be your half-brothers.'

'No, sir,' very decidedly.

'Then tell me the relation in which you think they stand to you.'

The girl raised a pair of honest eyes to his, and answered:

'Of course I can't tell, sir, exactly, but I think they are none of them any relation at all. Mrs. Calloran was a widow woman when my father married her, and her four sons are all Callorans, not Fermoys.'

' Then, in fact, there is no Fermoy but yourself ?'

' And Mrs. Fermoy, sir, as I told you.'

' Is she an Irishwoman ?'

' No, sir, English ; but her first husband was London Irish, like myself.'

' What is a London Irish person ?'

' A boy or girl born in London of Irish parents.'

' A very clear definition,' said Mr. Desborne with his pleasant smile, and then he glanced over his notes once again.

' It is a long way from Dublin to Kensington,' he said. ' How did it happen that your parents took such a leap ?'

' General Galvaine came to London, and they came with him. They were married at St. Mary Abbot's, Kensington.'

' You have not told me your Christian name, I think.'

' Aileen, sir—Aileen Anisia. I was called after Mrs. Galvaine ; she stood godmother to me.'

' When your father left Ireland had he any relatives living there ?'

'No, sir; not that I ever heard of. He had nobody belonging to him so far as I know, except an uncle that went out to America.'

'Was he a Fermoy also?'

'Yes, sir, Shawn Fermoy; if he is living, he must be an old man now.'

There ensued a pause, during which Mr. Desborne once again looked at his notes.

'Thank you,' he said at last. 'I do not think I need trouble you further at present, but I should like you to give me your address, in case I want to write to you.'

'I live at 14, Field Prospect Road, Battersea,' answered the girl; 'but please don't write to me there.'

'No?'

'They would all at home want to know who the letter was from—and I'd rather not, sir. If you would have the kindness to send a line for me in an envelope directed to Mr. Vernham, care of Messrs. Bricer and Co., Minories, I'd get it quite safe.'

'Is Mr. Vernham a relative of yours?'

'Of mine! Oh no, sir! He's a gentleman.'

The statement seemed to Mr. Desborne
odd, but he asked no question and made no
comment, only took down the address, and
said, 'Very well,' in a tone Aileen concluded meant that she might go.

She rose to depart, but stood irresolute,
evidently having something on her mind of
which she wished to disburden it.

'I hope, sir,' she began, 'you won't think
I am taking too much of a liberty; but why
did you want to see my father?'

Mr. Desborne looked at her as she spoke
as if he too had forgotten something he ought
to have remembered.

'When you read our advertisement, what
did you think it meant?' he asked, answering
her question with another.

'I could not think, sir. Mr. Philip—Mr.
Vernham, I should say—asked me if there
was anybody who would be likely to leave my
father money, and I could not call to mind
anyone unless General Galvaine. Then Mr.
Philip told me the General was alive, and

that perhaps father was wanted as a witness
or something of that sort, and I thought if
you didn't mind I should like to know.
You'll excuse me, sir.'

'There is nothing to excuse. It is most
natural you should wish to know, but at
present I am not able to tell you very much.
The matter is more in my uncle's hands than
mine. I may say, however, that it relates to
money.'

'To money, sir?'

'Yes; but you must not go home fancying
yourself an heiress.'

'I am not likely to do that, sir,' said
Aileen, in the tone of a person who felt there
was something sadly grotesque in the suggestion.

'Still, it seems to me probable something
will be coming to you, and, therefore, if a
small sum would be of any use at present, we
should be happy to advance it.'

'Thank you, sir, but I am not in need.'

'I think you had better have a few pounds.
You may wish to buy something; all young
girls'—he had been about to say 'ladies,' but

substituted the better word—'love to buy a new dress, do they not?'

'Many of them do, very likely,' she answered, flushing to her temples; 'but I have had other things to consider.'

'Well, consider a new dress now. Suppose I write a cheque for twenty pounds?'

'Indeed, sir, I am obliged, but I have enough gowns; and I would have come in a better'—here the flush grew deeper—'only I had to go to market, and——'

'I hope,' interrupted Mr. Desborne, 'you do not imagine I think the dress you wear other than most proper and suitable. Why I mentioned such a thing was because I often hear fashions in dresses talked about. Is not there any purchase you would care to make?'

'You are too kind, sir; but I do not want to buy anything, unless——'

'You need not tell me if you feel I am unworthy of confidence,' he rejoined lightly.

'It is not that, sir, and I would be quite wrong to take what you offer—because, sir, if there should be no money coming to me, how would I ever pay you back?'

' I would take my chance of that.'

' But I couldn't, sir. If not asking too much, though, five pounds would be a great help to me. I had saved up against the preserving time—for we get some good orders then from richer people than we serve in our regular round—but the money was taken.'

' How do you mean taken—stolen ?'

' It was not thought stealing, exactly ; but I'll never get it back again, all the same.'

' And are you sure five pounds will be sufficient ?'

' Yes, sir, it will do. I'll take that, if you are so good as to trust me, but no more.'

Mr. Desborne laid down five sovereigns, and watched the girl with a curious interest as she took out her handkerchief, knotted the money into one corner, laid that corner in her palm, drew a fold of the handkerchief between her first and second fingers, and wrapped the other portion round and round her hand.

As she finished this performance she chanced to look up, and, seeing Mr. Desborne's amused expression, a smile leaped into her eyes and spread over her face like a sudden burst of sunshine.

He laughed and said :

' I never saw that done before.　Will it be safe ?'

' Quite, sir ; it's the safest way of carrying money, unless in your mouth, and I never like to put it there, because I don't know who may have been handling it.'

' Do people ever carry money in their mouths ?'

' Oh yes, sir ! lots of the poorer sort who have holes in their pockets and no purses— and often no handkerchief, either.'

Mr. Desborne did not answer, for the excellent reason that he was unable to think of anything to say.

The incongruity between this girl's present associates and her future prospects ; between this struggling to-day and possibly brilliant to-morrow ; between that bandaged hand and the fortune its fellow-hand might hold, struck him all at once as something so pathetic and so out of all proportion, that he could only open a door leading into the hall and walk with her in silence to the step outside, standing on which he had first noticed her.

The poor as the rich know them, and the poor as the poor know them, are so very different, that when the curtain is lifted sufficiently even to afford a peep at the reality of their existence, it gives a greater shock to well-to-do folks than they care to experience.

Mr. Desborne's kindly face wore a much graver expression than usual when he re-entered his office, where he at once proceeded to write a note, which he directed to Philip Vernham, Esq., asking that gentleman to favour him with a few minutes' conversation at his early convenience.

CHAPTER V.

THE JUNIOR PARTNER.

IF Mr. Desborne ever wondered, as indeed he did more than once after their interview, whether Timothy Fermoy's daughter were quite straightforward; if it had occurred to him—still, in a speculative sort of way it was probably quite as well she declined, for reasons best known to herself, that twenty pounds offered in the pure kindness of his heart—the moment he saw Aileen's friend, Mr. Philip, all doubts vanished as completely as mists melt away before the sun.

There could be no conspiracy between them—he was evidently as straightforward as she—and all the sure faith Aileen had inspired, but which eight-and-forty hours managed

to put a little to the rout, returned with conviction.

'Yes,' Mr. Vernham explained, 'he had
known Aileen Fermoy since she was quite a
child. His father baptized her; Mrs. Galvaine stood godmother. These facts were
writ plainly in the parish register of St. Mary
Abbot's twenty-two years previously. He remembered Fermoy's shop in Kensington.
Been in it often when a small lad, and also
in later life. His parents dealt there. Fermoy was a pleasant, well-mannered, industrious, honest fellow, who had received some
education. Mrs. Fermoy was—but I cannot
speak about her, Mr. Desborne, as I ought,'
the young man broke off to say. 'She was
an unselfish, devoted, unworldly creature, who
tended my mother for six years with a love
and a kindness simply unimaginable. She
was to her nurse, friend, servant, sister,
daughter, all in one—I could never tell you
the extent of her affection, generosity and
delicate consideration. If we had been rich
as we were poor, great as we were of small
account, we could never have been treated by

her as we were.   It is no marvel I should do such little as lies in my power for Aileen Fermoy.   If I were able to give her thousands, no money could repay the debt of gratitude I owe to her parents.'

'Really, now, this is very nice,' commented Mr. Desborne, turning his chair a little so as more directly to face his visitor, who spoke with an enthusiasm all the more convincing because it was absolutely destitute of excitement.

His voice held a tone as though tears drawn from some deep fount of early sorrow were not very far distant; but his manner was quiet and full of the goodly habit of self-restraint.

Certainly, thought the lawyer, they were a curious pair, a very curious pair—a pair that interested him mightily, but also were a puzzle. He could not grasp the situation, and he scarcely saw his way to ask any question likely to render such an extraordinary alliance intelligible.

Mr. Vernham saw something of this embarrassment in Mr. Desborne's face, and hastened to relieve it.

'I suppose there is a legacy behind your advertisement,' he went on, 'and that you have sent for me to tell you all I know about Timothy Fermoy and his daughter. I may say, in a word, I know nothing but what is good of the Fermoys.'

'I am convinced of that; but, you see— well, to be plain, if everything comes out right there will be money—for this girl—and from the terms in which she referred to you, I thought I might obtain some further information without raising undue hopes in the mind of the person most interested.'

'Aileen is very practical,' commented Mr. Vernham.

'No doubt; but still she is young, and it would be cruel to excite her expectations only to disappoint them. It was for this reason I took the liberty of asking you to call, which I trust has not been an inconvenience. I had no idea you were so near Miss Aileen's own age. I imagined you were old enough to take a fatherly interest in her welfare.'

The young man looked at Mr. Desborne for a second with an expression in his eyes as

though he were not quite pleased, but finding
no cause for offence in the lawyer's face,
Aileen's singular friend answered frankly:

'I take as keen an interest in her welfare
as if she were my sister—keener, I think, because in that case the ties of blood would
modify much that I feel towards this girl. I
am aware it is nothing concerning me you
want to hear, but yet I can scarcely make
you comprehend the position in which I
stand to Aileen Fermoy unless I speak of myself.'

'Indeed, Mr. Vernham, I should be delighted to hear anything you have to tell,
always supposing the past is not unpleasant
to recall.'

'You mean if there be no painful story
in my life?' said the young man with a
smile. 'I am happy to assure you my past
has not a skeleton hidden anywhere—our
record is clean enough, I think. There has
been no worse stain than poverty—caused by
others—no more bitter grief than death.'

'What can be more bitter?'

'Disgrace,' was the reply. 'I hear of

troubles every day which I wonder men can bear and live.'

'Many men do not seem to have much difficulty in bearing troubles which leave health and pocket untouched,' said Mr. Desborne dryly.

'That is precisely what amazes me.'

'I gather that your father is or was a clergyman, Mr. Vernham?'

'Was—he died nearly fifteen years ago.'

'Then surely he must have known himself, and informed you, that the heart of man is deceitful above all things.'

'And desperately wicked,' finished Mr. Philip. 'Yes, I suppose he did know the fact in the same abstract way that we all do. Probably he thought there were wicked people at Mile End, or in the New Cut, or even a few streets distant from his own house; but I greatly doubt if he ever realized his next-door neighbour could be deceitful till he learned the fact from experience.'

'Ay, how was that?'

'Of course I do not mean exactly his next-door neighbour — but a great house, the

principal in which he and his family had
known and trusted for years.   All his money,
and he was fairly rich, was in the custody of
that house people considered as safe as the
Bank of England till it collapsed.'

'And he lost——'

'Everything.   I ought to tell you that
after he had bèen at St. Mary Abbot's for
five or six years he was appointed to a very
good living in Bedfordshire, which he had
held only for about twenty months before
Valleroys' crash.'

'Only fancy his being beggared through
Valleroys'!' commented Mr. Desborne. 'But
I beg your pardon—you were saying——'

'That even after they suspended payment
the public supposed a good deal would be
saved out of the wreck. I need not tell you
how affairs turned out. To end the story so
far as our part in it is concerned, at length
my father, worn out with anxiety, died, leaving us utterly destitute, save for a modest
annuity secured to my mother by an in-
surance he had fortunately effected in the
Scottish Widows' Fund.'

' Ah !' exclaimed Mr. Desborne.

' It was necessary to return to London, and as her income would only afford the most modest apartments, my mother wrote to Mrs. Fermoy, for whom she had always entertained a great respect and liking, asking if she knew anyone who had rooms to let at the required price. A reply came at once saying that the Fermoys would be pleased to let their first floor, and hoping she would not be offended at the suggestion. I do not think I need weary you further, Mr. Desborne. I am sure you understand now how it happens that I know so much of the Fermoys, and esteem them so highly.'

' Thank you ; I believe I understand perfectly. The only thing I am not quite clear about is how Timothy Fermoy's daughter happens to be in—in such an humble position, since, as I comprehend, her father sold one business and bought another, and was at no time in indigent circumstances.'

' That is quite true. He was always, for his station, well-to-do. After my mother's death I still continued to lodge in their house until Mrs. Fermoy was attacked with an illness which ended fatally, and, of course, I never lost sight of them. When Fermoy was in Guy's I used to go and see him as often as possible. Poor fellow! I am afraid he realized long before he went there that his second marriage was an utter mistake. He thought to secure a home and a friend for Aileen, but——'

'Is Mrs. Fermoy number two so very objectionable?' asked Mr. Desborne.

'There is nothing against her character, if that is what you mean,' answered the other. 'She means to be kind, she is good-natured and honest and sober, and all that; but it is a miserable home for the girl, and the chief burden of keeping it up lies on her. The present Mrs. Fermoy had a right royal time after Fermoy's death. She sold the goodwill and the carts and the horses and the stock all well, for she is a pushing, rather clever woman—clever, I mean, over a bargain —and while the money lasted she never asked herself where more was to come from.'

' It did not last long, I suppose ?'

' It did not. Then Mrs. Fermoy, who boasts she is " not one to sit with her hands in her lap when there is any work to do," found the house where they reside at present, with the little business attached, which her step-daughter manages. There is no absolute want, I hope, but Mrs. Fermoy's sons, the Callorans, are a sadly rough lot, and I have often wished Aileen could separate herself from them and take a situation as lady's-maid, or something of that sort. She is not badly educated, and would make a useful companion — I mean in an humble sort of way, of course.'

' Of course,' echoed Mr. Desborne, in an enigmatical tone.

' But the poor girl has an idea the household could not be maintained if she left it, and I do not like pressing her to take a course she feels wrong.'

' Quite impossible.'

' Should she be entitled to any legacy, however, her stepmother had better know nothing concerning it.'

'Miss Fermoy seems to entertain a precisely similar opinion.'

'I am glad to hear that, because whether the amount prove small or large—five pounds or five hundred—it would melt like summer snow in Mrs. Fermoy's hands.'

'Yes,' said Mr. Desborne thoughtfully. 'Yes.'

'Is there any further information I can give you?' asked the young man, breaking the silence which ensued.

'I think not, thank you. If there should be, I may take the liberty of writing to you again. You are in Bricer's house?'

'Yes—clerk.'

'And a letter will always find you if addressed there?'

'Or to my lodgings in Colebrook Row.'

'Who lives in Colebrook Row, if I may inquire?' asked a cheery, incisive voice at this juncture, and Mr. Vernham, turning round, saw a small man with gray hair and dark eyes, who, having entered by a door leading from the hall, and come

quietly across the room, had heard the words
which dictated his question.

'I do,' answered the young man, with a
grave and distant inclination of his head.

'And may I ask, further, if you ever see
Hope sitting there speculating on traditionary
gudgeons ?'

'I have not been so fortunate,' replied Mr.
Vernham, in the tone of a person humouring
some crazy fancy. As a matter of fact, he
concluded his questioner was deficient, not to
use a stronger word.

'Ah, you don't read Lamb, I see! Perhaps,
like many other young fellows, you think
him out of date.'

'I beg your pardon, I had forgotten.
Hope, so far as I am aware, does not reside
in Colebrook Row ; but if Elia were to return
there, I could take him to several places within
a stone's-throw of Cloak Lane where she
not only speculates upon gudgeons, but
catches them too.'

'Ay, indeed, and where are her fisheries,
if I may ask ?'

'In every city, town, and village of Great

Britain. There never were such fisheries before—not even in the time of the South Sea Bubble.'

'And Hope is represented by——'

'The modern promoter—who sits at ease in his office and angles through the post.'

'Humph! Have you fallen a victim to the modern promoter?'

'I have nothing to lose,' was the reply.

'Mr. Vernham's father was a sufferer through Valleroys' failure,' explained Mr. Desborne.

'I felt sure you were Mr. Vernham,' said the elder man. 'I am very glad to make your acquaintance. Many and many a pleasant hour have I spent in the company of a gentleman of your name.'

'Did you know my father?' questioned the young fellow eagerly.

'I think not. To the best of my belief, the gentleman I refer to died before your father could have been born. My friend, my cherished companion, is Abner Vernham.'

'My great-grandfather was Abner Vernham, but he has been dead nearly a hundred years.'

'Yes, but his books are not dead. They are upon my shelves, perfect mines of information. And so you are his descendant? How oddly things come round! And you have kindly called to tell us about the fair itinerant, or, more correctly, fair peripatetic.'

'Mr. Vernham does not understand your flowers of language, uncle,' interrupted [Mr. Desborne, noticing the sudden cloud which swept over their visitor's face.

'I do not quite understand,' said the young man with cold constraint. 'Though Aileen Fermoy's shop is but a small one, the girl is in no sense an itinerant.'

'He does not know,' thought Mr. Desborne; 'he has never seen her "dressed in character."'

'I expressed myself foolishly,' said the other Mr. Desborne, who, though older than his nephew, was junior in the firm. 'Fact is, I have never seen the young lady.'

'Aileen does not pretend to be a young lady; she has too much sense,' observed Aileen's friend.

'The young woman, then,' substituted Mr.

Thomas Desborne; 'my nephew has had that privilege, however, and I may venture to say he was greatly struck, not merely by her good looks, but by her good sense.'

'Is she good-looking?' marvelled Mr. Vernham, as if propounding the question to himself.

'In my opinion—not that that is worth much, of course—decidedly good - looking,' interposed the head of the firm.

'Well, perhaps so—possibly she is—but the idea never occurred to me that she had any pretensions to beauty.'

'You mistake; I did not say she was beautiful. I said she is good-looking, and I may add I consider she is better than good-looking. I cannot recall ever before seeing a face so honest, kind, and frank.'

'There I am quite with you,' said the young man.

'What further charm could be added to a woman's face than those my nephew has mentioned?' asked Mr. Thomas Desborne.

'I do not profess to be an expert,' was the reply; 'but I imagine a woman might be frank, kind, and honest, and yet seem very plain indeed.'

' You regard expression as nothing, then ?'

' I regard expression as a great deal. It is entirely her expression which makes Aileen Fermoy pleasant to look upon, as her mother was before her.'

' You knew her mother ?'

' Mr. Vernham has been explaining to me how he came to know the Fermoys so intimately. I am greatly indebted to him,' put in Mr. Edward Desborne, not sorry to give the conversation this turn.

' As I have mentioned, I am only too glad to be of the slightest service to Aileen Fermoy.'

' I feel so sure of that I do not apologize for having given you a vast amount of trouble,' answered Mr. Desborne warmly.

' Indeed you need not.'

' Putting Miss Fermoy aside for a moment, will you allow me to say how pleased I am to make the acquaintance of Mr. Abner Vernham's great - grandson ?' said Mr. Thomas Desborne. ' What an antiquary, to be sure !

By the bye, he was at one time curate of St. Christopher's, close at hand.'

'Well, hardly close at hand now,' corrected the younger man.

'Its site, its site!　I have an old engraving of the church upstairs.　Dear me! only to think that we should meet over this business of Timothy Fermoy's daughter!'

'There are Vernhams in Sussex——relations of yours, I suppose,' observed Mr. Edward Desborne amiably, anxious to give his visitor 'a leg up.'

'Of Vernham Castle?　No; they are not related to me.　Or, to put it better, I am not related to them.　They are of French extraction, I believe.'

'Came over with the Conqueror, of course,' said Mr. Abner Vernham's admirer, 'as, I suppose, your people did too.'

'No; according to my great-grandfather, we are Saxons.　I believe our name to have been originally Wirem or Wirenam.　Indeed, in some old deeds it is spelt indifferently Virenam and Verenam.　I have a curious paper written by my ancestor which proves that he at least had some reason for supposing we were here long before the Conqueror landed.'

' Ah, you beat us hollow there! We cannot trace a step further back than 1311,' said Mr. Thomas Desborne.

' But surely that is a very respectable pedigree ?' said the antiquary's great-grandson, with a polite smile ; ' and one which is probably a vast deal clearer than ours,' he added, in a spirit of proud humility.

'I cannot say much about the clearness,' confessed the other. ' There is a Desborne mentioned at the time Edward II. assigned the " favour of the city " to the mayor and aldermen—and then we hear little of the family till Ralph Desborne died of the plague in 1543, leaving large benefactions to the poor. Whether he was the direct ancestor of Fulbrick Desborne, beheaded on Tower Hill, from whom we can claim a straight descent, is somewhat doubtful. But I weary you, Mr. Vernham. I forgot the present generation lives too fast to take any interest in such old-world questions.'

' There is no question in which I take so

much interest as that of genealogy,' answered the young man.

'Your own,' thought Mr. Edward Desborne, but he kept silence, while his uncle said archly :

'I foresee, Mr. Vernham, that I shall very often have to ask you to spare me a few minutes' chat about Miss Fermoy's affairs.'

'As often as you please,' was the reply. 'I pass close by here frequently, and, even if I did not, I should only have to ask for leave to absent myself, and, as a rule, it would be granted.'

'You like Messrs. Bricer; you find them pleasant ?' asked Mr. Edward Desborne.

'They are very considerate.' After which prudent acquiescence Messrs. Bricer's clerk took his leave of uncle and nephew and passed out into Cloak Lane.

'Nice young fellow that !' remarked Mr. Thomas Desborne, when the office-door closed behind Aileen's Mr. Philip.

Mr. Edward Desborne did not answer. He was leaning back in his chair and tapping a gold pencil-case on the blotting-pad.

His uncle looked at him curiously.

' I said Mr. Vernham seemed a nice young fellow, Ned.'

' I heard you,' replied his nephew.

' What do you say ?'

' That I think he is a bit of a prig.'

' Prig !—how ?—why ?'

' Well, for one reason, because of the way in which he referred to our client.'

' In what way would you have him refer to her ? It appeared to me he spoke very nicely about the girl.'

' He spoke as if she were infinitely beneath him in rank.'

' So she is.'

' As if she were some lower order of creation.'

' Do be reasonable, Ned ! It isn't like you to take unjust views. The young man talked about this girl Fermoy just as a young man ought to talk about a girl in her station. His tone was respectful—appreciative, friendly— but not familiar. I must say I was very much pleased both with his words and manner.'

' Oh !'

The elder Desborne burst out laughing.

' I knew it !' he exclaimed ; ' I felt sure of it !'

' Sure of what ?'

' That at the precise moment I appeared on the scene you had evolved a very pretty little plot, with Messrs. Bricer's clerk for hero, and Timothy Fermoy's daughter for heroine. Here is a steady young gentleman, you thought, with no money—and there is a good young woman with too much ; and then you were vexed to find he looked on the young woman with the eye of cool common-sense, that he was honestly her friend, and not wrongly or foolishly her lover. I like very much to see you take off your hat to an old apple-woman, as if she were a duchess ; there is a former-day chivalry and gallantry about your manner to the sex which has its charm ; but in cool blood I suspect even you would not consider an alliance between a female costermonger and a clergyman's son a precisely desirable match.'

' She is not a female costermonger, and

she will be an heiress rich enough to be
run after by men of far higher rank than
your friend Abner Vernham's great-grandson.'

'Yes; but he does not know that, and if
he did I suspect it would not make much
difference.'

'No; because, as I said before, he is a bit
of a prig. From the moment he began talking
about his family I gave him up.'

'He did not say a word about his family
till you asked him if he were connected with
the Sussex Vernhams.'

'Who can only trace back to the Conquest,'
added Mr. Edward Desborne, with a satire
foreign to his nature. 'I do think a gentleman ought to wear his pedigree as he does his
clothes, without drawing public attention to
the subject.'

'And I think it the most proper and natural
thing in the world that a man should feel
proud of having come of an old stock.'

'I do not see that we, at any rate, have much
to boast of, even though our stock be old. Go
back as far as we will, we cannot claim kindred

with anyone more exalted than a London merchant.'

' Many an English nobleman can trace no higher origin,' retorted Mr. Thomas Desborne, with a flush on his cheek ; ' and better far to be descended from an honest merchant than from a profligate king and his light-o'-love. Forgive me, Ned ; I ought not to have said that. I am very sorry,' added the speaker, with a quick tinge of compunction.

' And I ought not to have said what I did,' returned his nephew impetuously. ' How foolish, wicked, I am! What is this girl, what is this young man, that they should cause me to vex you? You are sure I did not mean it. You know how much dearer you are to me than anyone except my wife ;' and Edward Desborne took his uncle's hand in both of his, and then stroked it with a tender, caressing affection unspeakably touching.

' I do know, Ned,' replied the other; ' but there is something you will never know, and that is how dear you are to me.'

After which remark there ensued a pause, during the continuance of which neither spoke.

Then the elder man disengaged his hand, and, taking up some papers he had brought with him into the office, he went upstairs, while his nephew looked straight out of the window at the backs of the houses in Queen Street, thinking perhaps of the disappointment he had been to the kindest uncle that ever lived.

CHAPTER VI.

MR. TRIPSDALE.

AFTER leaving Messrs. Desborne's offices, Mr. Vernham turned his steps, as Aileen had previously bent hers, towards Dowgate Hill.

Before he could reach that thoroughfare, however, he heard a sound as of someone hurrying behind him, so fast that, even while he moved aside to give the individual space to pass, he was surprised to hear the words, 'I beg your pardon, sir,' uttered almost in his ear.

Turning, he beheld a sight which surprised him—a youth wearing a gray felt top hat, lower in the crown and broader in the brim than fashion usually affects, a light tweed suit, a white waistcoat, a washing tie of a pale salmon colour, in which was jauntily

stuck a very sporting gold pin in the shape of
a horseshoe, ornamented with a pair of hunt-
ing crops artistically crossed ; not that Mr.
Tripsdale, for indeed it was he, and none other,
patronized the turf, but the accessories appealed
to his sense of beauty, and, as he tersely put
matters, ' If you do a thing at all, you ought
to do the whole thing.'

He had done the whole thing that day, and
this marvellous get-up was the consequence.

' Mr. Vernham ?' he said interrogatively,
raising his hat as he spoke.

Mr. Vernham acknowledged the soft im-
peachment, and waited for further information.

' In Messrs. Bricer and Co.'s house ?' gently
insinuated Mr. Tripsdale.

' You are quite right. May I inquire why
you ask the question ?'

' Merely for the purpose of identification,'
was the reply. ' It is somewhat awkward to
thank the wrong person.'

' You are right, and it is quite certain I have
done nothing to merit your thanks.'

' On the contrary, you conferred a great
favour on me last winter.'

'I!' exclaimed Mr. Vernham, amazed. 'To the best of my belief, I never saw you before in my life.'

'And your belief is correct. Nevertheless, the fact remains that you did me a kindness for which I feel extremely grateful; I accidentally heard a Mr. Vernham was with our Mr. Desborne, and thought J would wait outside on the chance of speaking to you.'

'But really I have no recollection of ever having served you in any way,' persisted the young man.

'That may well be; but I am detaining you, sir. If you will allow me to walk with you—pray excuse my freedom; I mean no offence—I can explain. You trace no likeness, I suppose?' And Mr. Tripsdale presented a full-front view of his face for inspection.

'Nature must have broken the mould,' thought Philip Vernham. 'She never surely would attempt to cast such another set of features.' But he only answered, 'I cannot at the moment recall anyone you resemble.'

'Ah!' exclaimed the other, evidently disappointed. 'Suppose we go down here.'

' It does not matter which way I walk, so long as I get to the Minories eventually,' agreed Mr. Vernham, who perhaps felt as well pleased not to have to pace Cannon Street in company with that cane, that pin, and that hat.

' Thank you. May I ask you to cast your memory back to the 27th of last December ?'

' I have done so, and what then ?'

' On the morning of that day you travelled from Godalming in a train which stopped at Weybridge, where a little fellow—little, though older than myself—got into the same compartment.'

' I remember him—a delicate-looking lad.'

' He is my brother.' The tone with which Mr. Tripsdale signed, sealed, and delivered, so to speak, this statement would be as impossible to describe as for any words to tell the pride, affection, and pleasure which pervaded voice and manner while he announced the relationship.

' Is he, indeed ? He interested me very much. I have often thought of him since then.'

'And he has often and often and often talked about you. Poor little chap! I don't know what he would have done if you had not paid his fare for him. He is such a sensitive fellow, his misfortune makes him — you know.'

'I noticed he was not quite straight.'

'No one could help noticing it, and that painful limp. It was a fall out of his nurse's arms injured him. But for that he would have been a fine tall man, taller than I am.'

The 'poor little chap' might easily have topped his brother and not been a giant, after all. But there was something so beautiful, so pathetic, in that brother's love for the young life shadowed, for the stalwart frame dwarfed, that only a cynic could have smiled at the contrast between the proportions suggested and the actual individual who instituted the comparison.

'I am so sorry,' said Mr. Vernham.

'You would be if you knew him well. He is such a dear fellow, but as a rule shy with strangers. He says he can't tell how it was he took so to you from the first. I wanted to call and pay you the money for him ; but no, nothing would do but he must go to Bricer's himself, and that was only because he hoped he might see you.   He didn't, though.'

' No ; I was out.'

' He found the ticket, after all, and they returned the money at Waterloo.'

' He mentioned that fact in his letter.'

They were past Calvert's brewery and All Hallows' Church by this time, Mr. Tripsdale so careful to give his companion the curb and to prevent his being jostled, that he walked in the roadway himself, at the peril of his life and to the danger of that tweed suit, which was never built to rub shoulders with the wheels of cabs, drays, and railway vans.

It was in vain Mr. Vernham entreated him to walk on the sidepath. ' I am doing very well, sir—very well indeed,' was the only answer he could elicit, and he felt quite a sense of relief when Messrs. Desborne's clerk elected to leave Lower Thames Street, and turn up that vile-smelling covered passage which con- ducts to St. Mary-at-Hill.

' There are only the two of us,' said Mr.

Tripsdale, pacing jauntily along, and keeping a distant eye on various quiet short cuts he meant presently to utilize.

‘ Yes, I gathered as much.   I hope your brother is getting on well with the wood engraving he spoke of ?’

‘ He is doing very well indeed, though that sort of work has gone somewhat out of fashion. He earns more than I do,’ finished Mr. Tripsdale, with the air of a person stating a fact he expected might be found hard of belief.

‘ Does he really !’ said Mr. Vernham, surprised, not because he supposed the honorarium paid by Messrs. Desborne for his companion’s services was large, but because he had somehow mistakenly jumped to the conclusion that a wood-engraver’s wage must be small.

Perhaps Mr. Edward Desborne had good reason for his remark about Aileen’s friend, who was inconceivably ignorant concerning many matters of which people who have knocked about the world know at least something.   When poverty enters the world’s lists clad in a complete suit of pride, the chances are against its making many friends, or of its learning to take a vast interest in the every-day, common, but often pathetically touching, affairs of its neighbours.

It was partly for this reason, and partly be-cause he had for years lived a self-contained, self-centred, and unnatural existence, that Mr. Vernham knew as little about the concerns of his fellows as any gentleman well could. While Mr. Edward Desborne was a sympathetic listener to the story of everyone's pains and pleasures, Mr. Vernham preferred, as a rule, not to hear anything concerning pains he was unable to relieve, pleasures in which he felt inclined to take no share.

'He does indeed,' said Mr. Tripsdale, gratified by his companion's evident astonish-ment, though happily unaware of its source. 'He is only a little fellow to look at, but he can turn out splendid work. Have you happened to see "The Dragon and Grass-hopper" wrapper?'

Mr. Vernham was obliged to confess he had not seen the wrapper in question.

'Well, then, you just should. It is on all

the stalls.   Do take a look the first time you have a chance.   No need to buy, you know. Gus cut the whole thing. Wonderful for such a young chap ! but that, after all, is not what his heart is set on.   He wants to be a regular artist.'

It would be utterly impossible to tell the triumph with which Mr. Tripsdale made this avowal.   It was as though he had said his brother desired to be Prime Minister or Commander-in-Chief, and meant to compass his ambition.

The whole thing seemed to Mr. Vernham infinitely touching ; all the more so because he did not believe the quiet, pale-faced lad who had been so distressed for the want of a few shillings was possessed of any talent beyond that of mere manual dexterity.

Delicacy of touch, quickness of perception, were qualities in which by reason of his very infirmity no doubt he excelled ; but the ability to engrave the work of others was one matter, while to conceive and execute work of his own was quite another.

'Has your brother talent, genius, then ?'

he asked, merely because he felt constrained to say something.

'Bless your heart, yes!' returned Mr. Tripsdale, falling into the familiarly-colloquial style, of which he had hitherto managed to steer clear. 'Excuse my rough speech, but I really could not help breaking out,' he went on. 'If you only saw the fancies Gus puts on paper! All out of his own head he makes the loveliest drawings. Often when I am in our office or running about the City I think to myself, How the deuce does he do it? Where does he get his notions? Poor little chap! and he is so contented and happy with it all.'

To the outward ear there was a want of relevance about this latter remark, but to Mr. Vernham's inner sense the connection of ideas was clear enough.

'I should like to see his drawings,' he said, moved by some influence, strange even to his own mind.

'If you knew how proud it would make him!' exclaimed Mr. Tripsdale. 'If you only heard what he has said about you over and

over again!   Of course, we are only two lads
in a poor way of life, and we never, except in
the course of business, have the chance of
speaking to a gentleman like you.   But that
is the reason why Gus dwelt so much upon
the notice you took of him, and the nice way
you talked—whenever your name comes up
his face lights all over.   I can just picture
him when I get home this evening.'

There is no wind of flattery so sweet as
that which blows soft and warm round some
unexpected corner ; and Mr. Vernham, being
very human, succumbed to the influence of
his companion's implied compliment.

We know how much more blessed it is to
patronize than be patronized.   To defend himself against the latter danger, Philip Vernham
had for years been going through the world
equipped in steel network which guarded him
effectually from all social assaults ; but when
those he considered inferiors approached him
properly, he covered this chain armour with
the manner of an ordinary mortal, and spoke
graciously to men and women who knew
' their places ' and refrained from familiarity.

For this reason he was liked much better by the porters in Messrs. Bricer's establishment than by his fellow-clerks, who thought him a ' stand-off ' and ' stuck-up ' chap, with nothing to support his pretensions.

This, indeed, chanced to be the trouble. There was nothing much in the young man of a saleable and serviceable kind. He had no marketable talent whatever. He was one of those honest, plodding, useful men, born by millions at a time, who are never likely to make a fortune, and who can only humbly assist others to make their fortunes. When his father lost his money and died, the young fellow's life was thrown utterly out of gear. Business was detestable to him: the mad hurry, the keen competition, the unscrupulous advantage too often taken, the constant watchfulness necessary, the continual precaution needful—all were hateful in the eyes of one whose choice would have led him to be a country clergyman and a modest scholar.

He had no gift whatever as the world accounts gifts. Ordinary abilities, a high sense of honour, a desire to do his duty both to God and man—of what use were these things to a clerk in Bricer's house? They did not give him five pounds yearly advance of salary. If he stayed with the firm till his hair grew gray he would never get a couple of hundred per annum from his exceedingly wise employers. He was worth no more than just what they paid.

A man under such circumstances must turn to some source of consolation.

Pride was the form Mr. Vernham's comforter assumed. With many men it takes the shape of drink. After all, an irrational pride is a safer demon to welcome into one's soul!

The demon was, however, leading Philip Vernham very safely as he listened to Mr. Tripsdale's words.

'Do you really think your brother would allow me to see some of his work?' he asked.

'Do I really think?' repeated Messrs. Desborne's clerk, coming to a halt exactly opposite the church of St. Mary-at-Hill; 'don't I really know it would be the happiest minute in his life? Because, mind you, he has

nothing to be ashamed of in his work. I
can't draw a line, but when I look at a paint-
ing or an illustration I know whether it is
good or bad, though I could not tell you
why. Gus's work is good—it is better than
good—and if the world ever gets a chance of
seeing it, the world will say the same.
Meanwhile, he can wait. If we were making
hundreds a year between us, I don't think we
could be happier than we are, though we live
on a second floor in Bartholomew Square.'

'Little Britain ?' suggested Mr. Vernham.

'Bless you, no ! that's Bartholomew Close.
We live in Bartholomew Square, Old Street,
near St. Luke's Church.'

'Why, I pass close by there twice a day !'

'Do you, now ? That's strange, too, ain't
it ? Well, sir, excuse the liberty I'm taking ;
if some time when you have five minutes
to spare you would call, I know you'd make
poor Gus laugh for joy.'

'But I am never near Old Street except in
the morning or evening.'

'Morning or evening, mid-day or at dead
of night, we'd be proud and happy to see you

in our humble home. It is humble, Mr. Vernham, I don't deny; but then, Lor', we couldn't be snugger or happier if we'd a mansion in Carlton House Terrace.'

'Possibly you might be less so,' answered Aileen's friend.

'I'm sure we would. You'd never believe how quiet that square is in the summer evenings when the children are gone to bed. We sit by the open window in the dusk, and fancy we're miles in the country. And it is better than any country to hear Gus talk about woods and meadows and rivers, water-lilies and such-like. I am not a great admirer of those out-of-London things myself, but I like to listen to Gus, for all that.'

'Are you not fond of the country, then?'

'No, sir, I am not; and it puzzles me how anybody else can be fond of such a place. Still, it is beautiful the way Gus tells how he was awoke by the birds each morning giving a finer concert than he ever paid a shilling to hear at St. James's Hall. But I'm detaining you, Mr. Vernham, and I ought to be getting back myself. May I say to my brother that you will come and see him ?'

'Yes,' answered the young man, with a little hesitation.

'Don't be afraid that we shall intrude on your kindness,' went on Mr. Tripsdale, noticing the hesitation and understanding its cause. 'We know our place, I hope, and how to keep it. Only Gus would take a visit as such a favour.'

'If so small a thing can please him, he shall certainly be gratified.'

'Thank you with all my heart and soul. And when, Mr. Vernham ? Don't put it off too long. Hope deferred—you remember.'

'I will try to look in to-morrow evening. Will that be convenient to you ?'

'As I said before, any day, any hour, you do us such an honour will be perfectly convenient.'

'Good-morning, then.'

'Good-morning, sir ;' and Mr. Tripsdale raised his hat straight in the air about six inches, put it on his head again, and without another word or look departed.

CHAPTER VII.

CHECKMATE.

Mr. Tripsdale went back to Cloak Lane as if treading on air, and entered the office with a manner of being at peace with the whole world, which, in a person of so remarkable an appearance, might have been accounted as infinitely humble.

It produced no impression, however, save one of irritation, on a man who was standing with his back to the empty fire-grate—a middle-aged, middle-sized, stiffly-built man, with short black hair, keen dark eyes, clean-shaven face, and broad, capable forehead.

'I have a word to say to you,' he began, addressing Mr. Tripsdale.

'Say on,' returned that irrepressible indi-

vidual, hanging up his hat and then standing at ease till the other should have
finished.

' It is this. The next time I find you lying
in wait for one of our clients, and ear-wigging
him, you'll go out of that door quicker than
you ever came into it—not to enter this office
again.'

' Oh ! you're head boss here now, are you ?
It is as well to know.'

' I am boss enough for that, at any rate,'
retorted the first speaker. ' You would not
have been here so long if Mr. Desborne had
listened to my advice.'

' I am quite aware of that, thank you.'

' Anyone but yourself might have rested
satisfied with insulting Miss Fermoy. You,
however, must in addition needs go and
chatter about her affairs to her friend.'

' How clever we are !'

' If you give me much more impudence I
will lay the whole thing before Mr. Desborne
the moment he comes in.'

' You will do that, anyhow.'

' Grin as much as you like, you will find

this morning's work turn out no laughing matter.'

'Well, well, shut up now! If I am to be hung, drawn and quartered, at least spare me an oration;' and with this remark Mr. Tripsdale was about to exchange his out-of-door coat for one which hung on a peg close to where his adversary stood, when that individual, in an access of wrath, exclaimed :

'You—you mountebank! How dare you disgrace a respectable office by wearing such clothes! You look more like a clown at a circus than a decent clerk.'

Mr. Tripsdale left the pepper-and-salt coat he had been about to take down still hanging on its accustomed peg, while he turned and faced his opponent.

'What is the matter with my clothes?' he asked, casting an affectionate glance over his new suit. 'They are a precious sight better than yours—and they are paid for, which, if all I can hear is true, Mr. Knevitt could not truthfully say about his.'

'You infernal young liar! what do you mean by that ?'

' Fish and find out,' was the cool reply. ' You know so well what Mr. Vernham and I were talking about that you will have no difficulty in learning what the talk is about you.'

' I don't owe a penny in the world.'

' That is what you say.'

' No one can say anything else.'

' What is the disturbance ?' asked a voice at this juncture, and, looking round, both the disputants beheld Mr. Edward Desborne, who had just returned, surveying his belligerent clerks with grave and annoyed surprise.

Mr. Tripsdale did not speak. ' It was not my place,' he explained afterwards to Mr. Puckle, for which reason he contented himself with ' watching the case.'

As for Mr. Knevitt, he was in such a white heat of rage that he could not for an instant find words to answer.

' Have you been quarrelling ?' went on Mr. Desborne, in a tone almost of incredulity.

Mr. Knevitt involuntarily moistened his parched lips with the tip of his tongue. Mr. Tripsdale, still watching his own case, continued to maintain an impartial silence.

'I had occasion to find fault with this young fellow,' said the elder clerk at last, 'and he answered in the most impudent manner.'

Mr. Desborne looked at the offender, who pleaded neither 'Guilty' nor 'Not guilty,' only in silence sucked the tip of the office ruler as though smoking a calumet. He was reserving his defence.

'You see, he will not speak, sir,' added Mr. Knevitt, in explanation and accusation.

Still Mr. Tripsdale kept silence.

'What was his offence, Knevitt—something heinous, eh?' asked Mr. Desborne. 'It must have been—you were talking so *very* loud.'

'He accused me of being in debt, and I do not owe a farthing in the world.'

'You ought to be a very happy man, then,' observed his employer.

'I am a very happy man,' returned the clerk, with an expression which belied his words. 'But, happy though I may be, I do not intend to put up with impudence from a lad like that.'

' He called me a mountebank, sir,' said Mr.
Tripsdale, with a graceful wave of the ruler,
' and found fault with my clothes.'

' What is wrong with his clothes ?' asked Mr.
Desborne kindly, rejoiced to think the young
clerk's sin was of no more deadly nature.

' Why, sir, only look at them ! I wonder
what your honoured father would have thought
had I ventured to appear before him in such
motley——'

' Things have changed a good deal since you
first came to my father, Knevitt,' answered
Mr. Desborne kindly ; ' and as for Tripsdale's
suit, I dare say he will find it very cool and
comfortable during the hot weather.'

' But you have not seen his hat, sir,' persisted Mr. Knevitt. ' Put it on.'

Like many amiable people, Mr. Desborne
was not blessed or cursed with a keen sense of
humour. Had he been, the spectacle of Mr.
Tripsdale, with his arms held stiffly to his
sides at ' attention,' and a martial frown on his
brow, scowling at Mr. Knevitt from under the
shadow of that broad-brimmed gray hat, must
have proved irresistible.

'Rather Quaker-like, perhaps,' said Mr. Desborne, 'but it too, doubtless, proves pleasant wear on a sunny day, such as this, for instance.'

'Will you please tell Mr. Knevitt now, sir, to put on his hat for you to see,' said Mr. Tripsdale, with an air of aggrieved dignity.

'It is not necessary,' answered Mr. Desborne. 'I know Mr. Knevitt's hat quite well ;' and he moved as if to go, when the managing clerk detained him.

'I hope you do not imagine, sir,' he began, 'that the matter in dispute between us had anything really to do with dress. That was merely a side issue—the other affair is much more serious. Had Tripsdale received my warning as it was meant, I probably might not have troubled you ; but his impertinence leaves me no choice. I have a most grave complaint to make against him.'

'Pray, then, let us hear it at once,' said Mr. Desborne impatiently.

'When he heard Mr. Vernham was with you to-day, his interest seemed so much excited

that I confess I felt surprised; but as he often
is excited I thought no more about the matter
till, on turning out of Cannon Street on my
way back from Abchurch Lane, I saw this
promising youth walking down Dowgate Hill
by the side of Mr. Vernham, and talking to
him in the most confidential manner. Their
conversation lasted—for I felt it was my duty
to follow—till they parted by the Lantern
Church. They were a long time together—
made many pauses, and spoke, as I could see,
eagerly, no doubt on the subject which brought
Mr. Vernham here.'

Mr. Desborne looked vexed.

'I am sorry,' he said. 'It is very strange.
It sounds very unpleasant, but it may be
capable of explanation. Is Mr. Knevitt correct
in what he tells me, Tripsdale, or has he made
any mistake?'

'He is quite correct in many respects, sir.
I did wait outside till Mr. Vernham left you,
and I did walk with him to St. Dunstan's in
the East.'

'Had you any previous acquaintance with
the gentleman?'

'I never had the honour, sir, of seeing Mr. Vernham till to-day.'

'You see, out of his own mouth he stands condemned,' remarked Mr. Knevitt eagerly.

Upon hearing which observation, Mr. Tripsdale thrust the ruler again between his teeth, as if resolved nothing further of an incriminatory nature should proceed from the source indicated.

'He may not have been talking, however, about Miss Fermoy,' said Mr. Desborne, amiably anxious to find some loophole of escape for his erring clerk. 'Were you, Tripsdale ?'

The young fellow shook his head.

'Don't you believe him, sir,' exclaimed Mr. Knevitt, eagerly translating the shake as a falsehood for the benefit of all whom the matter might concern. 'I know all about it as well as if '—'I had been down him with a light,' the senior was going to say, but substituted 'I had heard every word of the interview' just in time. 'Remembering how impertinent he had been to Miss Fermoy, he thought to make all right by currying

favour with Mr. Vernham, and telling him
the amount of her fortune and other particu-
lars you deemed it best to defer mentioning to
the lady.'

'Live and learn,' muttered Mr. Tripsdale,
sotto voce.

'What do you mean by saying Tripsdale
was impertinent to Miss Fermoy? I trust
you are labouring under some mistake.'

'Not at all, sir—not at all,' answered Mr.
Knevitt briskly, feeling he was now walking
on solid ground. 'When the lady called he
insulted her most grossly. Did not he, Mr.
Puckle?'

'Oh, come now, draw it mild!' expostulated
Mr. Puckle under his breath, but otherwise he
made no reply, good or bad.

Mr. Desborne looked at his subordinates as
if unable to believe the evidence of his senses.

'I really am astonished,' he said, 'not only
to hear that Mr. Tripsdale so far forgot himself
as to be rude to any client—more especially a
woman—but to find the circumstance was not
reported to my uncle or me at once.'

'Well, sir, you see, we do not care to make

mischief,' exclaimed Mr. Knevitt, a little crest-
fallen.

'*You* do, at any rate,' retorted Mr. Tripsdale, turning upon him ; 'and I did not insult
Miss Fermoy ; I did not say a disrespectful
word to her.   Did I, Mr. Puckle ?'

Poor Mr. Puckle—keeping one watchful eye
on the door in order to intercept the entrance
of any stranger, and the other turned in the
direction of Mr. Knevitt, who refused to see
his mute appeal—found himself in a very tight
corner.

He, at all events, not intending to make
mischief, had only told Mr. Knevitt about
the Whit Tuesday incident that morning,
as, sooner or later, an adverse fate compelled
him to tell Mr. Knevitt everything ; therefore he was quite unprepared for the violence
of the storm now pelting about his ears.
Driven to desperation between Scylla and
Charybdis, the unfortunate man answered :

'It was not exactly what you said, of
course, but the way you said it.'

Mr. Tripsdale was quite shrewd enough
to grasp the length, depth, and width of his

perilous situation. Puckle was not going to stand his friend, so he could only fight as one who has no ally.

'I confess I chaffed her,' he admitted, with the air of a prince pleading guilty to chucking a chambermaid under the chin; 'but I meant no harm, and how could I know her for other than what she seemed?'

'What do you mean by saying you "chaffed" her?' asked Mr. Desborne, with a sternness unusual to his manner.

'Nothing wrong, sir, I assure you upon my sacred word and honour. It all happened this way. Let Mr. Knevitt say what he likes. She—Miss Fermoy—came in here the morning after Whit Monday—a very awkward morning indeed—asking to see Mr. Desborne. She would not give her name or address, or state her business, and it was not my fault if I took her for a barrow girl. You did yourself, Mr. Puckle.'

'Don't appeal to me,' exclaimed Mr. Puckle; 'I took her for nothing, and answered her according!'

'You see, sir,' said Mr. Tripsdale, apologetically triumphant, 'I hope you will not think I am taking a liberty if I venture to suggest that probably, when you met Miss Fermoy, it did not occur even to you that she was connected with the Upper Ten Thousand.'

'It did not,' answered Mr. Desborne, overlooking the freedom of Mr. Tripsdale's remark in his desire to deal justly; 'but she was a woman, and as such entitled to all courtesy.'

He paused. A total silence ensued — then :

'I will overlook the grave fault you have been guilty of on this occasion, but must warn you to be careful in your conduct for the future,' he added, before entering his own office, the door of which he closed, leaving the three clerks together.

Without hesitating for a moment, Mr. Tripsdale walked to the door and knocked.

'Come in,' said Mr. Desborne. 'Oh! it is you, Tripsdale, is it? I really think you had better not say anything more——'

'I must say something more, sir. I can't

sit down patiently under Mr. Knevitt's accusation without uttering a word in my own defence. He has long been wanting to get his knife into me, and——'

'That will do, that will do!' interrupted Mr. Desborne. 'You had every chance given you of offering an explanation, and it was your own fault that you refused to give one. I cannot re-open the question.'

'Sir—Mr. Desborne—you have been always fair to me. I know you will be fair now. I could not and would not defend myself from such an accusation with Mr. Knevitt, who is always down upon me, standing by. I have never told you an untruth, I am not in the habit of telling untruths; and I assure you solemnly that Miss Fermoy's name was never mentioned between me and Mr. Vernham. Till Mr. Knevitt stated the fact I was not even aware Mr. Vernham knew her. I waited for him outside, I admit, and spoke to him, but only to express my gratitude for an act of kindness he did my brother, who is—delicate.'

'I am sorry, Tripsdale, you felt unable to say this earlier.'

'You don't believe me, sir—will you ask Mr. Vernham? He would tell you the same. As for talking about office affairs out of the office, I have never done so ; honour is honour, and a clerk may possess as keen a sense of it as an archbishop.'

During all the years Mr. Desborne's firm had been privileged to pay Mr. Tripsdale a salary, the head of it had never heard that individual make so long a speech, his answers usually being well-nigh confined to the Scriptural 'yea' and 'nay'; and it may at once be said the speech did not produce a good impression.

'I shall certainly not mention the subject to Mr. Vernham,' Mr. Desborne returned coldly. 'I am willing to take your word in the matter, and only wish you could have given an equally emphatic denial to the charge of having treated Miss Fermoy with discourtesy.'

'I did not mean to be discourteous, sir, and I don't think I was—exactly. I chaffed her, certainly, but not in the way you suppose. I should think very little of myself if I spoke disrespectfully even to a gutter girl.'

'Clearly understand in this office I expect civility to be shown to the poorest and lowest creature who walks the London pavements. If I hear another complaint of your behaviour I shall have to speak more severely.'

'But, sir, I was civil, only I talked perhaps a little over her head, and I am sorry for it—very sorry.'

'That is sufficient; do not let such a thing occur again. Now we will say no more concerning this unpleasant affair;' and Mr. Desborne made a sign of dismissal which the offender felt bound to obey, though his heart was full to overflowing of unuttered explanations.

It was so full, and he felt his employer's reproof so keenly, that without addressing one word to Mr. Puckle, who looked up as though expecting some communication, he went straight to his desk, and indited the following epistle :

' Honoured Sir,

'As it is obvious that I have had the misfortune to lose your confidence, I feel there is but one course open—namely, to resign my situation, which I now do, and with your kind permission will leave as soon as you have found someone to fill my place more efficiently.

'Your very obedient servant,

'Reginald Tripsdale.

'To Edward Desborne, Esq.,
    'Solicitor, Cloak Lane.'

It must not be supposed that this business-like 'notice to quit' sprang into life from Mr. Tripsdale's brain in the perfect form presented. Many sheets of office notepaper were spoiled ere the above result was arrived at, a fair letter written, and a true copy made.

After these things were done, the communication for Mr. Desborne placed in a directed envelope, and the duplicate folded up and placed in his own inner pocket, the young clerk laid all the ' waste ' in the empty grate, set a match to it, and watched till not

a tell-tale atom remained behind; then he
knocked again on the panel of his employer's
door, and waited. No answer came, so he
went in, left the note where it would be
seen immediately anyone entered, and came
out again, with the look of a person who
has passed the Rubicon, and is, though
determined, sorry.

He was very sorry. He thoroughly
realized what he had done. He had never
been in another situation. ' Desbornes' was
home to him,' as he mentally put it—' board,
lodging, washing, and fuel;' and now he
would have to search for the wherewithal
to provide those necessaries elsewhere. He
would have to consort with strange people
and get into the ways of unfamiliar offices, and
—which was worse than anything—he would
be obliged to tell his brother what had happened—that brother whom he tried to spare
as a mother might her child.

His heart was very sore and heavy within
him as he seated himself again on his stool,
and resumed the work he had left in order to
waylay Mr. Vernham.

'Much of a row?' asked Mr. Puckle, whose curiosity would not allow him to refrain from questioning any longer.

'No, "dismissed with a caution,"' answered Mr. Tripsdale airily.

'What were you writing that brief about, then?'

'My own business,' was the reply.

'You might tell me.'

'I might, but I won't. I am not going to tell you anything again, ever.'

'Please yourself.'

'That is just what I intend to do.'

Time went on, and as it went Mr. Tripsdale's heart grew heavier. He worked like a very demon in his endeavour to kill thought, and, leaving Mr. Puckle to answer all inquiries, devoted himself to making up arrears in a manner which amazed his slower companion.

It was when he was most deeply engaged that Mr. Knevitt entered, and, throwing a letter down on his desk, said:

'Take that to Chancery Lane, and bring back an answer.'

' Take it yourself,' retorted Mr. Tripsdale ;
' I am not your ticket-porter.'

Mr. Knevitt looked at him for a moment,
with the expression of one longing for a
fight, then picked up the letter and left the
office.

' You are doing it effectually,' observed
Mr. Puckle, who could not see such things
done and keep silence.

' Doing what ?'

' Cutting your own throat.'

Presently there sounded a muffled whistle.

' Yes, sir,' replied Mr. Puckle, whose desk
was close to the tube, to which he immediately applied his ear.

' You are wanted upstairs,' he observed to
Mr. Tripsdale, taking his ear from the tube.

Mr. Tripsdale descended from his stool,
and, marching out of the office defiantly,
mounted to the first floor, where he found
Mr. Edward Desborne and his uncle.

His own missive was lying open before the
latter gentleman, who said in a calm, dis-
passionate tone :

' Tripsdale, we have decided to return this

letter into your own hands, and I will tell you why. If we allow you to go, we must state the reason to anyone that may apply to us, and it would do you harm. Do not be foolish—do not allow your temper to get the better of your judgment. We are all liable to make mistakes, and the best thing to do is to try to avoid making them in the future. Now you can go,' with which curt dismissal Mr. Tripsdale was departing as meekly as a lamb, when the speaker added : ' Oh, just one thing more. Look through your wardrobe this evening, and try to find a suit better adapted for City work than the one you have been wearing lately. That is all.'

Mr. Tripsdale went out and stood on the landing speechless with rage—stood biting his nails savagely, and lifting one foot and then the other, in a desperate effort to refrain from executing a war-dance.

' Checkmate, by Jove !' he muttered, ' checkmate.' He was quite clever enough to grasp the situation instantly. ' If *I* give *them* notice,' he thought, ' they will say I left in a fit of temper because I did not like my dress being interfered with; and if I don't put on different clothes, *they* will give *me* notice. Hang it all! I can't throw up my berth over a summer suit;' and he slowly began to descend the staircase, grasping the baluster-rail tightly, as if it had offended him. 'Never mind, Mr. Knevitt, never mind!' he finished. 'My day will come, and when it does I won't forget you—oh dear no!' which mental exclamation afforded him so much satisfaction that he went down the remainder of the flight in double-quick time, and re-entered the clerks' office in the character of 'Richard is himself again!'

CHAPTER VIII.

A STRANGE INTERIOR.

When Philip Vernham on the following evening entered Bartholomew Square, the first person he saw was Mr. Reginald Tripsdale, clothed in sad attire, and quite in his right mind.

'I thought you might have a trouble in finding our number,' he said, raising his hat ceremoniously, ' so took the liberty of waiting about for you. Gus wanted to come and wait about too, but I would not let him. He is not over-strong;' after which utterance he relapsed into silence, with the view of permitting Mr. Vernham's fascinated gaze to wander over the beauties of Bartholomew Square.

'I did not imagine there was such a quiet

nook hidden away here,' remarked that gentleman.

'It is a curious thing, and one I have often noticed,' answered Mr. Tripsdale, pacing along with the air of a guide personally conducting some prince of the blood through a strange country, 'that no matter how well a man knows his London, he never knows it thoroughly. It is a city of surprises. Why, even I, who know its nooks and corners as well as I do my alphabet, am always coming across something new. It was only the other day I tumbled over, as I may say, six dolls' houses—alms, you know; such tiny bits of places, with green cottage doors, flowers in the window, and all the rest of it, just at the back of Moorgate Street—that I had never seen before. This way, if you please, sir ;' and, indicating an open door, he escorted his visitor up two flights of stairs, and, entering a front room on the second floor, exclaimed :

'Gus, who do you think this is ?'

A young fellow with a pale, sweet face came shyly forward, and said :

'Mr. Vernham, is it really you ?'

That was all, but his eyes were beaming with joy, and the hand he offered trembling with pleasurable excitement.

'Where will you sit?' asked the younger brother, as their visitor stood silent, vainly searching for something to say. 'Where will you sit?' with the satisfied air of one who feels he owns a vista of 'marble halls' and hundreds of 'vassals and serfs to command.'

He had noted the effect their second-floor front produced on Mr. Vernham, and felt wild with rapture.

'Thank you, anywhere,' replied Aileen's friend, taking the nearest chair. 'What a delightful room this is! You must forgive me for making such a remark.'

'You think it really passable?' said Mr. Reginald Tripsdale.

'I think it really lovely,' was the reply.

'It is all his doing,' declared the elder brother.

'It is all Gussy's doing,' affirmed the other.

'I do not know when I saw such beautiful old furniture,' observed Mr. Vernham.

'Got for a mere song,' explained Mr. Reginald Tripsdale. 'Mind, though, it was not like this when we bought it. The way we did the trick — but possibly I weary you, sir?'

'On the contrary, I am immensely interested.'

'When we came here just six years ago, we had nothing but a few cane chairs, the table you see'—indicating a heavy oblong oak table, black with age, standing on legs that looked like thick ropes, loosely twisted, rising from an under framework of the same pattern—'and the chair you are sitting on, which I hope you find comfortable.'

'I do, indeed,' and Philip Vernham got up in order to view the piece of furniture in question, which was exceedingly tall and straight in the back, and even more remarkably nobbly and corded about the legs than its friend the table, and seemed, moreover, afflicted in every possible joint with chalk stones. 'A divine chair—a chair for Art to rave about!'

'After Gus got into regular work,' proceeded Mr. Tripsdale, ' and my salary was raised a bit, the question arose whether we ought not to begin to furnish. We both thought it would only be right, but our views were different. My view was the walnut-wood suite ; Gussy's wasn't, so he undertook to " educate my taste." This is the result.'

' You could not have a more charming result,' said Mr. Vernham, looking round a room wainscotted in oak up to about three feet from the floor, and above divided into panels, the centres of which were painted a cool, subdued colour, while the dividing portions matched the wainscot. In each division hung an ancient engraving or piece of quaint embroidery, and the whole effect, if not in accordance with the canons of true art, was pleasantly like art, and sufficiently suggestive to remind an onlooker thankfully of modest old-world homes, where lavender-bags scented the linen-press, and all fragrant herbs and useful cordials found their place in the housewife's cupboard.

' I can't say those nobbly things are exactly my style, even after all the time Gus has spent upon educating me,' proceeded the younger brother; 'but I don't think them as strange as I used to do; and as I see the same sort often in pictures, I suppose it is quite right. We've had an enormous amount of fun over our house-furnishing, anyhow—we've been to all sorts and sizes of places, and met with many queer characters. Down at the East-End, among the small dealers, we picked up most of what you see for as many shillings as we should have paid pounds west of Holborn. Often we hired a truck and brought them home ourselves, had them scrubbed, and then set to work to put a new face upon them. The samplers and worsted pictures we sent to the cleaner. Polly says we ought to be burnt out, so as to clear all this rubbish away, but I don't see that myself. I like to look at the things, if only to remind me of the nights we walked through Bow and Bromley and Stratford, keeping our eyes open. Why, this room is as good as a diary to me—that is the way I put it to Polly—but, bless you, there is no convincing women!'

'Is Polly your sister?' asked Mr. Vernham.

' My sister-in-law who is to be,' amended Mr. Tripsdale.

' Indeed ! is that so ?' And Mr. Vernham looked at the elder brother, who remarked with a smile :

' According to Reggie. I think, however, he had better marry her himself.'

' My future wife's name will not be Polly, but Success,' declared Reggie, with an emphasis which surprised the visitor. ' I shall woo no bride except Miss Getting-on-in-the-world. I mean to make money—lots of it— and you, Gus, must win fame and carry on the family.'

' And how do you propose to make lots of money ?' asked Mr. Vernham, really interested at last.

' Well, sir, I don't mean to remain a clerk all my life. There will be some money coming to us one of these days—it does not depend on anybody's caprice or will that can be fought over, but it must come on to Bartholomew Square when our great-grand-aunt retires from this world to a better. I am sure I don't wish anyone to die ; but, still, when an old lady has had the enjoyment of money for over seventy-five years, and can find nothing else to do in life save sucking her gums, which have long been toothless, I say it is time for her to take a front seat in heaven, where none of the family believe they will ever meet us.'

' Why ?' asked Mr. Vernham.

' First and foremost, because we must have two thousand pounds ; second, and as a sort of clincher to the first, because Gus is going to be an artist and I a lawyer ; and third, in the way of " summing up," because we are both too uppish.   Just fancy poor Gus " uppish " ! '

' I can't, really,' said Mr. Vernham with a smile.

' You see, our great-grand-uncle, who probably knew his wife better than most men, forecasting what would happen, left his money to her only for life.   After his death she remarried almost immediately, and had a large fine family ; and you may imagine there would be a nice complication were the money at her disposal, which it is not ; and that is what makes all her sons and daughters so mad.   In the ordinary course of nature our father ought to have had that two thousand pounds years and years ago; but the old lady held on. When I think of all the good he could have done for himself and others had she slid off when she was about sixty, I feel inclined to doubt whether Providence takes so accurate a view of family affairs as might be wished. Gus tells me I am wrong, and that I ought not to say such things; but I can't think I am so very far out, after all.'

'You are,' said the elder brother, with more firmness than Mr. Vernham could have given him credit for—'you are indeed, Reggie. Supposing anyone had spoken in that tone about our father, how should you have liked it? Besides,' he added, with a twinkle in his eyes, 'to put the matter on no higher ground, it is foolish to say such things. We had, figuratively, the old door shut in our faces in consequence of a similar speech; and Elder Farm was a pleasant place to go to,' at which thought the lad sighed. Some persons' lives do not hold the memory of so many pleasant places that they can see one closed to them without regret.

' It is a pleasant enough place, especially about Christmas time,' confessed Mr. Tripsdale, manifestly disconcerted by his brother's statement. ' Gus got his taste for old oak there,' he continued, addressing their visitor. ' Lord! you should see the kitchen fireplace, with dogs and settles round, and great pots that might have served Jack the Giant-killer's host to boil his victuals in. There are cupboards in that house, and buffets and arm-chairs, I am told, that could not be matched in England, and Gus is right enough. I did say what slammed the door in our faces, and yet it was not much, after all. An old gentleman last Christmas year began maundering about the fine voice our great-grand-aunt rejoiced in when she was a girl, and I could not help saying, as our great-grand-aunt had rejoiced in such a voice so long ago, " I thought it was high time for her to secure a permanent engagement in the Celestial Choir," which chance remark, of course, went round the family like wildfire, with the result Gus indicates.'

' Well, of course it was not quite nice,'

persisted the elder brother; 'anyone hearing such a remark might have imagined you wished her to die.'

'That was just what she said, and, when I declared I hoped she would live to dance on our graves, told me I was telling—well, she put it forcibly—lies.'

'I suppose she was pretty nearly right,' observed Mr. Vernham.

'No; I don't want her to die. She is welcome to live another hundred years for me; but I should like some of that money before Gus and I arrive at an age when we can do nothing but suck our gums and make ourselves disagreeable.'

'People can make themselves disagreeable at any age. It is not necessary to be seventy-five to do that,' said Gus.

'I had better change the subject, perhaps,' returned his brother, with a good-tempered laugh. 'Show Mr. Vernham some of your fancies, Michael Angelo. Now, don't be shy,' he added. 'You order him to open his portfolio, sir. He will do what you tell him.'

'I should like greatly to see a few of your

sketches,' began the visitor, who, having noted with dismay that an abundant tea was laid for three persons, had been considering for some time how he could most easily and quickly effect his exit. 'I am rather pressed for time; but if you could favour me with a peep at your drawings, it would gratify me very much.'

'Please do not talk of running away yet, sir,' interposed Mr. Desborne's clerk, 'or I shall think I have frightened you with my foolish talk. You must have tea somewhere, Mr. Vernham, and Gus and I hoped you would excuse our freedom if we asked you to have a cup with us. As I said before, you need not be afraid of our intruding. We are not people who want to take an ell if anyone gives us an inch, but we should esteem it an honour if you would have your meal here.'

'I should be a churl if I refused,' answered Mr. Vernham, immeasurably relieved, for he had been expecting the advent of Polly, or someone else equally objectionable; and to know the lads had kept faith with him, and spread a feast solely in his honour, seemed pleasant to the man so few, so very few, delighted to consider.

'We thank you,' said Mr. Reginald Tripsdale, with the air of a Grandison, 'though it is only what we might have expected. Now, Gus, look alive!' he went on in a quite different tone; 'produce your wares and show your samples; at last a judge is going to inspect them!'

'Indeed, I am no judge,' declared Philip Vernham very earnestly; 'I do not know much about pictures. I only know what I like.'

'Precisely my case,' was the reply. 'I know what I like, and that is Gussy's work. We are not always at one on the old oak question; but when he gets among the trees and the fairies, I say nothing can beat him, and you'll say the same, sir, or I'm a Dutchman.'

'Reggie, why will you trouble Mr. Vernham about my poor sketches?' remonstrated Reginald's brother; 'I am sure he cannot——'

'I am sure he can and will,' interposed

Mr. Tripsdale. ' Do you suppose he ever would have come here only to listen to our babble ? Well, if you won't show him yourself, I will.'

CHAPTER IX.

MR. TRIPSDALE'S ASPIRATIONS.

'Just come here, Mr. Vernham,' and Mr. Tripsdale led the visitor behind a screen which shut the farther window off from the rest of the room, making an apartment within an apartment, which, though only furnished with a small table, an office chair, an easel, and a stand containing flowers, seemed delightfully quaint and charming. 'This is where he does his engraving,' said Reginald, indicating the table, 'and there he puts his fancies on paper,' indicating the easel.

'Is that fancy?' asked Mr. Vernham, pointing to a portrait which seemed to smile sadly at him as he stepped within the screen. 'What a lovely face!'

'No,' answered the artist, who had followed

the speaker, with a face more flushed and a gait more tardy than usual. 'I forgot I had left her there. That is Reggie's sister-in-law who is *not* to be.'

' She is very beautiful.'

' It is not a bit like her,' said Mr. Tripsdale. ' She laughs at it herself. Who wants a wife with such a die-away, broken-hearted look as that girl has ? I just think I see Polly going about the streets wearing such a hat and such a Norah Creina dress, and carrying a bushel measure full of water-lilies in her arms. " No, you wouldn't catch me making such a guy of myself," she said the other day. Here is the real Polly.'

Philip took the photograph presented to him and examined it curiously. The likeness was that of a comely, good - humoured, practical sort of girl, with regular features and a peculiarly decided and determined expression pervading her appearance. Her dress fitted like a glove ; there was not a crease or fold about it. Her fringe was carefully curled, and the remainder of her hair piled scientifically on the top of her head.

Not a lock was out of place, not a plait in her gown but looked as if it had been constructed with the aid of a plumb-line. Every button of her bodice came out clearly as though each had been touched up separately. She was a good type of the London girl of her period in the class to which she belonged — self-satisfied, capable, industrious, hard, honest, able to take care of herself, and possibly of others; but she was not the girl who smiled mournfully from the easel, with a wistful tenderness Polly's face had never known.

Yet Philip Vernham could trace a likeness, a subtle, indefinable likeness which seemed wonderful to him. The maiden who held those fair water-lilies still dripping from their river home, who had every grace of form and face, the pliant figure, the soft suggested movements the old artists understood so well, that give an added charm to the fairest woman, never could have resembled that smart, tidy, well-dressed, conscious Polly the photographer's skill had reproduced with such cruel accuracy; but still there was

a likeness, which might have been of the
spirit imprisoned within the buxom Polly's
fleshly tabernacle.

'I do not understand where you got this
girl,' said the visitor, after a long, wondering
look at the face, which seemed mystified also.

'I got her from Polly,' answered the
painter.

'Yes—but——' And Mr. Vernham hesitated.

'Have you never seen, when talking to
some friend, an expression quite unfamiliar
come into his countenance and change it?'

'I have—an unpleasant expression,' answered the visitor, at which reply Mr.
Reginald Tripsdale laughed appreciatively.

'Ah! when you have been arguing or
quarrelling, perhaps,' said Augustus Tripsdale,
who had forgotten his shyness in that earnest
belief in his art which carries true workers
over 'brake, bush, and scaur.' 'But that
is not what I mean. When sitting quietly,
you and a friend together — you and he,
perhaps, not even speaking—have you never
noticed an expression sweep across his face,

a look leap into his eyes, or some unwonted feeling part his lips, which changed him for the moment almost into another person ?'

Philip Vernham shook his head.

'You must have seen,' persisted the other, 'but perhaps you did not notice ; that is the difference between artists and most people. What I mean is, sometimes a window generally closed and curtained seems suddenly to be flung wide, and the soul looks out for a moment—the soul as God made it, which has got housed, to our thinking, unworthily. You do not understand me yet, I see. Well, I will put the case differently ;' and the bright, clever eyes and the eager, sensitive face were turned to the noncomprehending visitor, while Reginald Tripsdale exclaimed delightedly :

'He is on his hobby-horse now, Mr. Vernham. After all, Gussy, I am not the only one in the world who is unable to follow you.'

'Mr. Vernham will follow me presently,' returned the lad whose soul had found so poor a mortal lodging. 'Have you ever,' he went on, addressing their visitor, ' seen some rough, untutored fellow stretched on a bed of sickness, ill unto death ? No ? Then what am I to do ? How shall I explain ?'

' Just talk on,' suggested Mr. Vernham ; ' tell me what you have seen and thought, and though I am very dense, no doubt I shall grasp your meaning presently.'

' It is I who am obscure,' said the young artist humbly ; ' but I will try to be plainer, for I should like you to think with me. I said a minute ago some rough, untutored fellow, and I have seen that, too ; but what I had particularly in my mind was a rough, loud-voiced, coarse-featured Irishwoman, the least lovely creature externally I ever beheld, though possessed of a heart of gold. When she lay a-dying I went to see her, and I never was so amazed. Coming death had succeeded in effacing all the hard lines a hard life had graven on her face. Her skin was like that of a little child, the wasted hand she held out was soft and white as the most delicate lady's, and in the eyes I remembered so dull and weary there shone the light of

God's eternal peace. I have seen in dying
people that marvellous change over and over
again.'

Mr. Vernham stood thoughtful. He was
considering. He was better born, better
bred, better nurtured than the youth who
spoke. He was the son of a clergyman.
Such sights as Augustus Tripsdale talked of
ought to have been familiar to him, yet he
had never seen the things referred to. Was
he of those who having eyes see not, and
having ears hear not? A very serious
question to propound to himself in the case
of any man, and doubly serious in the case
of such a man as Philip Vernham, who had
hitherto gone through the world little satisfied
with other people, while much, though unconsciously, satisfied with himself.

'Your idea is,' he at last said slowly,
'that most men have two natures—one which
their fellows see, and another of which an
occasional glimpse is only caught.'

'Yes, that is my idea,' agreed the young
fellow, pleased at being understood so far,
and confident Mr. Vernham would grasp the

further belief involved in his fancy when he
thought the matter more fully out.

'And you saw this face,' indicating the
lovely maiden with such sad, tender eyes,
'looking out of Miss Polly's open window ?'

'No, I won't go so far as that,' answered
the artist. 'If I had,' and he stopped, but
Philip Vernham comprehended he might but
for his brother's presence have added, 'I
should have tried to win her.'

'I saw something which inspired the
picture,' he went on, feeling the pause
awkward. 'I am so glad you like it.'

'Indeed I do,' said Mr. Vernham.

'As a fancy sketch it is all very well,' interposed Reginald Tripsdale ; 'but for practical
purposes, for a good daughter, a capital
manager, a shrewd young woman, a jolly,
sensible, companionable girl, give me Polly; no
nonsense about her, no die-away, lackadaisical
rubbish there—a practical, useful, helpful,
economical girl, Mr. Vernham, just the wife to
keep things together for a foolish, dreamy,
clever young idiot like Gussy. Whenever

she has ten minutes to spare she comes here
to keep him straight.'

'She does,' said Gussy, 'and I often wish
she would keep away. If she would come
when you are at home I should not mind, but
she does hinder me so.'

Here was a state of innocence which Mr.
Vernham surveyed in dismay—a nineteenth-
century Garden of Eden before the Fall that
seemed impossible to his sophisticated imagination.

A buxom, healthy, capable young girl paying
visits to a solitary young man all alone!
lecturing him, advising him, making love to
him, no doubt. Truly there were things in
London a good deal beyond 'his' philosophy.

'She has always been like a sister to us,'
explained the younger brother; 'she blows up
our charwoman, mends our linen, interviews
our laundress—we could not get on without
Polly. How the deuce she finds time for all
the work she gets through I can't imagine.
She nurses her mother, who is delicate ; keeps
her father straight, who is an old fool ; sees
to her young brothers and sisters, and really

runs a lodging-house in Claremont Square, which keeps the family. No wonder Gussy's "beauty" disgusts her. With a face like that at the head of affairs the family would be in the Bankruptcy Court within a twelve-month. But all this is outside Gussy's work. Look here, Mr. Vernham.'

'Do you mean to say you have evolved all these sketches out of your own imagination?' asked Philip Vernham fifteen minutes later in that, to him, eventful evening.

'The ideas "yes," the adjuncts "no,"' was the reply. 'The scenery is all taken from the Upper Thames; the "little people" and their doings *came to me.*'

'How do you mean "came to you"?'

'Precisely what I say. You do not know the lovely notions which come to me when lying awake at night, while Reggie is like Miss Flanagan in the Irish ballad, "sound asleep and snoring."'

'I beg to say,' interposed Reggie with dignity, 'that I lie awake o' nights also, considering my future position as Solicitor-General.'

' He sleeps like a top, Mr. Vernham.'

' So would you, if you had as much on your mind as I have on mine,' was the quick if inconsequent retort.

' Well, as I haven't, I lie awake,' answered his brother, ' and see many things here feebly reproduced. Then I see the trembling leaves; I see the water-lilies springing up after fairy feet have pressed them ; I know why the grass by the river's brink looks trampled in the morning, and who has gathered the wild-flowers in Runnymede overnight. I could tell you where the good people have been holding high festival, and mark the precise spot where the witches last met.'

Philip Vernham looked at the speaker in amazement.

Were such fancies possible in Bartholomew Square, where dwelt tailors, bootmakers, watchmakers, and such-like ?

Could genius dwell there too, and lie awake o' nights garnering its wondrous fantasies ? It seemed so, though the fact appeared incredible.

' Come and have some tea, Mr. Vernham,'

said the practical Reginald. 'After that lot of idealism I should think you must be hungry. I hope you will like our tea. We get it from a friend in the trade. Those strawberries grew in a market garden down east, where the proprietor lets Gus gather for himself. The cake and ham are of Polly's providing, so I need say nothing about them.'

'Is it not very early for strawberries?' asked the visitor.

'Yes, rather, I imagine,' answered Gus, who was careful not to say those he had bought were forced, and then they sat round the table, Reginald acting as host, and the meal began.

It was a much better meal than Mr. Vernham would have had at home. The rate of exchange in London, as between landlady and lodger, tells heavily against the latter, and even if this were not so, how is a man to pay for his rooms, light, fire, and dress out of thirty shillings a week, and live luxuriously on the balance left?

Yet the Tripsdales on their joint incomes managed to live well and save money also.

' While my aunt, that is, our mother's sister, lived,' remarked Reginald, ' she was house-keeper to a wine-merchant whose stores and offices were in Norton Folgate, and we had leave to stay there with her.   When she died Gus and I had many a talk about what we ought to do. We felt we could not stand lodgings, furnished or unfurnished.   My aunt's illness and funeral had eaten up her little savings, and even when we sold her few possessions, all except the articles I indicated some time ago, there was still a deficit, which we paid off at so much a week out of our earnings.'

' Reggie paid it, Mr. Vernham ; I was earn-ing almost nothing then.'

' You have earned plenty and paid plenty since,' said Reggie, with a courtly wave of his hand ; ' but, as I was observing, we had many a talk about the best course to pursue.   The remuneration of a lad in a lawyer's office is never princely, and I may say at once we found that a very hard winter ; two or three times we were in an exceedingly tight place. It so happened I had to come into this square, and as I looked round me I saw chalked on

the window of this very room, " To let." Well,
to cut a long story short, we took it the same
evening, and moved in next day. That was
how we began housekeeping, with one room,
doing for ourselves ; now we have three rooms
and a charwoman to tidy up, and feel, I assure
you, as grand as though we had chambers in
the Temple, and an old laundress to manage
that our tea did not last too long, and all the
rest of what is called respectability. We could
afford now to take real chambers in one of the
smaller Inns, but we have got fond of
Bartholomew Square, and think it better to
save our halfpence than spend them. Gus is
in one building society, and I am in another ;
that is not a bad way of putting money by.
Mrs. Pring may live to grace Elder Farm for
half a century yet, and if Gus is to go to
Rome, and I am to become a solicitor, we shall
have to save a lot of pennies.'

'Are you going to Rome ?' asked Mr.
Vernham, turning to the young artist.

'Some day, perhaps,' he answered.

'Some day—no "perhaps" at all,' interposed Reginald. 'I can wait awhile for my

chance. I do not mean him to wait one hour beyond the time we can see our way clear.'

'And you really intend to be a solicitor?'

'I do. It is not precisely what I should have chosen; but I have thought it all out, and believe the calling to which my taste would have inclined me would not do. Certainly it would not do.'

Messrs. Desborne's clerk looked so portentously mysterious as he made this statement that Mr. Vernham did not pursue the subject, but continued to do justice to Miss Polly's choice of ham.

'I am sure Mr. Vernham would like to know the calling you would have preferred, Reggie,' suggested Reggie's brother.

'There is no reason why Mr. Vernham should not be told,' answered Reginald, with dignity; 'but the matter is one which could scarcely interest him.'

'I feel very curious,' declared the visitor; 'and if there be really no secret——'

'None in the world so far as you are concerned. I should not take the mass of mankind into my confidence, but you, of course, are different ;' and there ensued another pause, while Mr. Vernham waited for the information which did not come.

' May I tell ?' asked Gus.

' Of course, though there is nothing much to tell.'

' Reggie would like to be a detective,' said the other.

' A what ?' exclaimed Mr. Vernham, really thinking he could not have heard aright.

' A detective,' repeated Gus, speaking very distinctly.

' If you remember,' observed Mr. Reginald Tripsdale, ' I said it would not do, though what little talent I possess does lie in that direction. I felt it would not do. No more useful individual than a skilled detective walks this earth. Yet there is a prejudice against him. The way I put the thing in my own mind was this, " You may be indifferent concerning the world's opinion, but you have no right to pull down your brother, who is going to rise high," so I gave up my fancy.'

' You really believe you have the detective

gift ?' suggested Mr. Vernham, by way of saying something.

'Believe ! I know I have. You remember the Chingford murder, which has baffled the police for more than a year, and will baffle them for many a year to come ? Well, sir, that affair is no mystery to me. I could lay my hand on the murderer to-night.'

'Then why do you not ? It was a dreadful affair.'

'There is a lady in the case,' replied Mr. Tripsdale mysteriously — 'a lady who was very badly treated. Couldn't add to her trouble—pretty creature, too !'

'I think you were right in deciding the profession of a detective would not suit you,' remarked Mr. Vernham with a smile.

'Too soft-hearted, eh ? Well, perhaps so; at any rate, in this case I could not give up the criminal to justice. It was a mere look, a glance, gave me the clue, which I followed till I held the whole puzzle in my hand, and there it is going to remain.'

Philip Vernham's sense of humour was about on a par with that possessed by Mr.

Edward Desborne, otherwise Mr. Tripsdale's
frowning face, Mr. Tripsdale's dramatic ges-
tures, and Mr. Tripsdale's heavily impressive
manner, must have moved him to shouts
of laughter. As it was, he sat looking in
amazement at the amateur Fouché, who,
gratified at the impression he had made, continued :

'But even in my own profession this gift
will stand me in good stead. I intend to
make criminal practice my speciality. I mean
to carve my name on the topmost branch of
the legal tree, just as I mean Gussy to write
his high in art ; and, of course, this power of
tracking guilt home to its lair will be an
enormous weapon in my hand when I come
to cross-examine.'

'Of course,' agreed Mr. Vernham, over-
powered.

'But why should I weary you, sir, with
these fantastic visions ? Let me give you
another cup of tea. Do you like the scent of
that mignonette, or is it too strong for you ?'

'Not at all ; I wondered what the delightful perfume was.'

'Gus says we ought rather to have a jar of rose-leaves instead, to match the furniture, but we have no rose-leaves, and I don't know where to get any; besides, as Polly very truly remarks, if we begin having everything to match the furniture, we shall never stop till we are ruined. *Pot pourri* is very troublesome to make, she hears, and expensive, too.'

'When I have time I will make some myself,' observed Augustus.

'I think you might rest well content with the mignonette,' ventured Mr. Vernham.

'Particularly as Polly bought it,' added Mr. Tripsdale.

'If I am any judge of faces,' thought the visitor, 'that is the very reason he does not appreciate the perfume.'

'Three years ago a friend sent me a young myrtle,' he observed aloud. 'It has grown very much, but to my regret never yet bloomed; perhaps it may this season.'

'I can tell you why it does not flower,' said the elder Tripsdale eagerly.

'Indeed, I should like greatly to know.'

' The slip was not taken when the myrtle was in bloom, which it ought to have been— at least, so I am told,' was the explanation that elicited from Reginald the exultant remark :

' Knows a little of everything, doesn't he, sir ?'

' It seems so,' answered the visitor ; and really when, an hour later, he rose to take his leave, he felt convinced Augustus Tripsdale knew more than a little of many things.

' He has such a lot of time for thinking,' observed his brother. ' He is not like me, in a whirl all day long ; but I try to keep my eyes and ears open to pick up all I can, and then in the evenings we sit by the window in the twilight and talk. Lord ! what talks we do have !'

' You must find them very pleasant. You have a delightfully quiet home here, and a happy one, I am sure.'

' Yes,' returned Reginald ; ' I often think that when Gus is President of the Royal Academy and I am Solicitor-General, we shall look back to the old home and the days we spent in it with regret.'

' Time brings gain and time brings pain,' quoted Augustus sententiously ; ' we can't have one without the other.'

' If not intruding, will you allow me to walk a few yards with you, Mr. Vernham ?' said Reginald Tripsdale, when their visitor was at the door ; ' just as far as the City Road. I should take it as a kindness, and can perhaps show you a short-cut.'

They went down the staircase together, and out into the quiet evening. Some children were still playing in the square, but most of them had gone home, and silence was settling down upon the place.

' I am going to ask you a favour, sir,' began Mr. Vernham's companion, without any needless beating about the bush. ' It is this. If you ever have occasion to come again to our office, will you speak to me just as you would to any clerk ? I mean as though this evening had not been ; and should Mr. Desborne chance to mention my name or ask whether you are acquainted with me—I don't

say he will, but such a thing might happen
—would you mind telling him the service you
did my brother, but not that Gus is as he is?'

'Mr. Desborne does not know, then?'

'And I don't want him to know. He is so
kind he would not rest until he got him under
some specialist, or maybe into some hospital,
and we don't care to be befriended and
meddled with. Personally, I think philan-
thropists are the greatest nuisances on the
face of the earth. They are so anxious to do
good they can't let people alone, and they
can't understand that people, as a rule, don't
care for good to be done them.'

'Is Mr. Desborne a philanthropist?'

'He is, sir, and a deuce of a one, if I may
use such an expression. I don't mind,
though, who he exercises his benevolence
on so long as he keeps his hands off Gus. I
know we are neither great nor grand, but we
have our feelings, for all that. We don't
want to be patronized, and we are not going
to be patronized, either. Now, this is your
shortest way home. Good-night, sir, and
thank you. Good-night.'

CHAPTER X.

HOPE DEFERRED.

IT was a broiling day in the early part of August. Pea-picking had long been over in the market farms that stretch so far into West Middlesex and Surrey, into Kent and Essex, and along the winding Lea, Isaac Walton's own river, to wooded Hertfordshire; and the men and women who had gathered hundreds of thousands of bushels for that gigantic householder, London, and afterwards stripped the gooseberry and currant bushes, were even then filling great baskets with ' black Jacks,' egg, Orleans, and greengage plums, and, in favourable localities, even early William pears, than which, if it be not a libel to say so, no fruit that grows can taste less like fruit.

The last Bank Holiday also of the year, the very last universal holiday till Christmas, which, as it has always been, is not accounted a holiday at all, was past and gone, the ' small fruit ' had been gathered, brought into market, bought, sold again, eaten, and preserved, and Aileen Fermoy sat once more in her shop alone, knitting stockings.

If she were reviewing her season's earnings, she had no reason to feel dissatisfied. The debt to Mr. Plashet had long been repaid, and the five pounds lent by Mr. Desborne also. Mr. Philip had taken the amount to the firm and returned her the firm's acknowledgment. So far all was well, yet, judging from the expression of her face, things were not well with Aileen Fermoy.

Things, on the contrary, were extremely unpleasant. True, trade had been, and trade was, as good as trade could be. Each day brought fresh customers, because a pleasant face, nice manners, and honesty cannot fail to draw custom in any business. She was doing, commercially, very well, very well indeed. The Field Prospect Road business bade fair to become a good business, but of what use is prosperity, especially to a woman, lacking that sweetness which, according to the Scriptures, makes even a dry morsel palatable?

She would have been more than content with the driest morsel could she but have eaten it in peace. She did not yearn for wealth or greatness, she was willing to earn her bread in the sweat of her brow; what she did pine for was some quiet place in which to partake of her modest crust.

But the trouble was, she knew that never for ever could she hope for quiet in a house where her father's widow dwelt—Mrs. Fermoy herself was always ' on the go,' as were her many sons, and as also were her grandchildren. For Aileen to ask for rest in that home was as useless as asking for rest on the treadmill or an express train. Imagine a quiet horse who knows his business doomed to run in double harness with a skittish colt off the moors, and some idea may be formed of the life poor Aileen had to lead.

Because, though old enough, Heaven knows, to pace through life soberly, Mrs.

Fermoy was, to all intents and purposes, a young colt ; and what can possibly be more unsatisfactory than the sight of an elderly matron, who should be staid, possessed by the insane idea that she is a good deal younger than any girl ? And the worst of Mrs. Fermoy's delusion was that it proved expensive.

No woman, young or old, can go 'junketing ' about among her friends unless she have many sixpenny-pieces in her pocket ; and when pecuniary matters revert, as at some time or other they must do, to 'first principles,' it becomes an extremely nice question who is to supply the sixpences.

Aileen had supplied them till she grew tired and heartsick, when the usual trouble ensued.

After a person has unfailingly given sixpences to many people who asked for them, any refusal to continue the supplies is considered as a breach of faith.

It was so considered in this case, but Aileen remained firm. She had made up her mind during Whitsun week to contribute no more

than a certain amount to the family ex-
chequer, and she held to her resolve spite of
many bitter reproaches and cutting taunts.

Dick, having spent his unjustly-acquired
five pounds, had returned hungering and
thirsting for more. Most unfortunately, he
failed to receive the justly due chastisement
promised by his elder brother, who, being out
of work, and for the time dependent on his
mother, was forced to listen when Mrs.
Fermoy intervened on her favourite son's
behalf, called Tom a brute, begged him to
look after his own children, and ' dared him '
to lay a finger on any of hers.

After this episode Dick was particularly
requested to partake of an excellent tea, and
did so willingly, making for his own con-
sumption many rounds of toast, which he
buttered hot with that liberality people often
evince when distributing goods they have not
had to pay for; while Aileen maintained a
dignified silence, and was reproached by her
stepmother because she ' could not find a
pleasant word to say to the poor fellow who
had come back to them at last.'

'But who has not brought with him the five pounds he stole,' answered the girl.

'Oh, come now, don't let's have any talk of that sort!' cried Mrs. Fermoy. 'Stole's an ugly word, and, after all, the paltry money never went out of the family.'

'It went where I do not intend any more to go,' said Aileen.

'Why, bless my soul! anybody to hear you talk might think you had lost a five hundred pound bank-note!' retorted Mrs. Fermoy.

'In its way the loss seemed as great to me as five hundred might to another.'

'Lord pity you! If you take things to heart that way, you won't have much of a life, I'm thinking.'

The remark was so true, even while so foolish, Aileen felt it best to hold her peace, and drank her tea in silence, although Dick, seizing a favourable opportunity, derisively put out his tongue to its full length.

Even that delicate attention did not affect her as it might once have done. 'Those who laugh last laugh best,' and there was something in the look which rewarded his grimace that made Dick feel uneasy. In truth, Aileen had decided there was to be no more pilfering. A woman whose husband could not work by reason of an accident, and who had many small children to support, lived close by, and to her care evening after evening, week after week, Timothy Fermoy's daughter carried her money to be kept safely.

The amazing honesty of the poor justified her trust. There were times when that half-starved and anxious creature did not know where or how to get a loaf; yet to the extremest farthing she returned Aileen's deposit, and received with pathetic thankfulness the sixpence or shilling the girl gave her for the care.

After a time, when compelled to absent herself, Aileen paid this woman to take charge of the shop, which arrangement proved a grievous offence to Mrs. Fermoy, but a great gain to Aileen, who speedily found out how many sixpences had been taking wings to themselves and fleeing away, perhaps after that hoarded five pounds so unscrupulously annexed by Dick.

For these reasons, and also because the season had been a peculiarly favourable one, Aileen, as she sat and knitted, might have been justified in considering herself a fortunate girl, but she did not do so.

A great hope had at Whitsuntide sprung into life, and though she tried not to think about or depend on it, quite unconsciously she had thought till time first obscured its rays, and then blotted them out altogether.

No one can hope without expecting, and this girl had gone on expecting hour after hour and day after day till she felt nothing good could come of the matter—that she must put the notion of external help out of her life if she were to do any good in it.

' I'll try to save a little and follow Mr. Plashet's advice,' she said half aloud, as she laid one stocking aside to begin another.

Now, Mr. Plashet's advice had been given in this way : ' I'd have thought a sensible, hardworking girl like you would have tried to better herself before now.'

' And indeed, sir, there's nothing I would

like more than to better myself if I only
knew how.'

' Well, a round in Battersea and the
Borough Market may be all very good as a
start, but you ought by this time to be working up a business in some of the new suburbs
and dealing with a man down the road.'

' Down what road, sir ?' asked Aileen
humbly, anxious for information.

' Down any road, to be sure. Wherever
there is a road out of London, market gar-
deners send their carts along it. You could
buy just as cheap from them as from me, and
then your goods would be left at your own
door instead of your having to fetch them.
I'd think that over if I were you.'

Aileen did think it over, and even mooted
the notion to Mr. Philip, who failed to look
on the project with enthusiasm.

' You see, sir,' went on the girl, a little
chilled, but not wholly disheartened, ' if any
money came out of that advertisement ;' and
she paused as if expecting an answer.

' It is difficult to tell, but I think money
may come out of it.'

' And how much do you think, sir ?'

' I really cannot conjecture.'

' Do you suppose it would be more than twenty, sir—the gentleman offered to let me have twenty.'

' Yes, I should imagine more than twenty.'

' If it mounted to fifty——' tentatively.

' If it did, what then ?'

' I'd try to get out of this.   I'd find a shop —a regular shop, I mean—somewhere.   Mr. Plashet says I might let the upper part for enough to clear the rent, and I'd take Jack, and allow Mrs. Fermoy what I am giving her now.   I know I could make off a living, and, oh ! I should think I was in heaven if only I could be left to earn my bread in peace.'

Mr. Philip looked at her gravely.

' You must not be disappointed, Aileen, if Mr. Desborne finds he has made a mistake.'

' Indeed, sir, I am expecting nothing.'

' I think you are wise, and I think you would do well to put this idea of a shop also out of your mind, else it may unsettle you a little.'

That it had unsettled her a good deal there could be no doubt.   The days passed on, the weeks, the months, and it was somehow a different Aileen who sat among her stores counting the number of her stitches.

The heat was oppressive ; spite of the open field beyond, the whole neighbourhood seemed pervaded with what has been aptly called that ' poor peoply smell ' which the sun or damp muggy weather draws out of the very ground in those parts of London where the rank and file of its inhabitants dwell.

An indescribable smell, one which may be felt !   Outside the shed two of Mr. Thomas Calloran's children were sitting on the curb with their feet in the gutter.

Parental fondness or foolishness had purchased for the boy a toy trumpet, from which he was producing ear-splitting sounds, for the delectation of Field Prospect Road.

The girl, who was a little younger, naturally wished to produce similar sounds, and earnestly entreated, ' Let I blow the trumpet, do, Bertie !'

' Na—h, ye wan't blow the trumpet, ye wan't blow the trumpet !' returned the other, emphasizing his words by digging his elbow into his sister's ribs. 'Hoo-to-to!' and he blew a blast of derision on the abominable instrument, above which rose wails of distress from Minnie, caused partly by pain—for Bertie's elbows were sharp—and partly by disappointment.

Aileen rose and went out. Mrs. Fermoy's grandchildren were brats no human being except a prejudiced parent could have really liked; but Aileen had a soft heart, and the poor little girl looked so miserable and neglected—with great tears running down her dirty face—that Timothy Fermoy's daughter was moved to deep compassion.

'Why, Minnie dear, what is the matter?' she asked, gingerly picking up the child, who was indeed almost too grimy to touch.

'He won't let I blow the trumpet,' sobbed Minnie.

'Why can't you let your sister have it?' said Aileen, looking down at Bertie.

'Na—h, she sha—an't blow the trumpet, she sha—an't blow the trumpet!' drawled this scion of the Calloran house. 'It's mi—en;' and he blew a blast and pulled a face which made Aileen long to shake him. Clearly Dick's mantle had fallen on his nephew. 'Never mind, Minnie,' remarked Aileen; 'we will find something nicer for little girls to play at than blowing trumpets. What have you been doing, child?' she added suddenly; 'you are as black as if you had been up the chimney.'

'I did that,' said Master Bertie proudly, suspending his musical performance in order to make the statement; 'there was a sweep's brush standing outside Mrs. Dingland's, and I ran away with it and painted Minnie's frock; didn't I, Minnie?'

'Iss,' answered the child.

'Very well, Bertie, we'll hear what your father has to say about such doings.'

'Who cares for him,' retorted Bertie, 'or for you, either? Hoo-to-toot-too!' and the wretched trumpet gasped out its last breath in one husky scream of defiance.

'There, now you have broken it,' said the young imp. 'I'll go and tell my fader, I will;' and, full of this intention, he ran into the family mansion, where the eldest Mr.

Calloran was, spite of the heat, sitting in the kitchen before a huge fire placidly smoking his pipe, while a pewter measure stood on the table beside him.

Second thoughts being best, Bertie said nothing about the trumpet then. Instead, he clambered up the paternal knee and exclaimed, ' Give me a drop, fader ; do give me a drop.'

' That's my fine fellow,' returned the proud parent ; ' you ain't afraid of honest ale : take a pull, lad ; you know the trick : that's the way. Why, I'm blowed if you have left as much as would drown a fly. You'll soon be able to toss off your half-pint like a man ; that'll be a rare bit to tell Aunty Ally.'

Which seemed so delightful a joke, one so likely to amuse and gratify Aileen, that the burly father laughed till tears came down into his eyes, and Master Bertie echoed the laugh with a shrill ' He, he, he !'

There ensued a pause—a pause of some minutes—during which the father was considering that before long his precious son would be old enough to fetch a pot from the Bedford Arms, close at hand, and wishing

that desirable time had arrived ; while the
son, who, ere so very many years had elapsed,
might be depended on to give good support
to the nearest and many other 'pubs,'
thought in a childish, cunning way whether
he had not better fasten the guilt of breaking
that toy trumpet on nasty Aunt Ally at once,
when Aileen herself entered—Aileen, yet
another.

It was the same Tom Calloran who sat
smoking ; it was the same wretched little
Bertie astride his father's knee, who sat
there thinking in his childish way ; but it
was quite a changed Aunt Ally who, pushing open the kitchen-door, walked straight
to the fire and thrust a sheet of paper deep
among the glowing coals.

'Hillo !' cried Mr. Thomas Calloran, 'a
love-letter.   Ha, ha, Miss Ally !'

'Are there no letters but love-letters ?'
asked the girl, bending a perfectly colourless
face over the blaze.

'There may be ; I don't know. I never
had many letters in my life, and I've always
done my courting by word of mouth.'

'If ever I have a love-letter,' said Aileen, 'I do not think I shall put it in the fire.'

'When you have one, girl, I hope it will be the right sort,' answered Mr. Calloran, in the character of a stern moralist. 'Ally, could you lend me a shilling?' he added, as a natural afterthought. 'I'll pay you back honest whenever I get a job.'

'I will *give* you a shilling,' answered Aileen, with an emphasis which implied she had often before lent money and failed to get it back.

'You don't seem to give it over-willingly,' said Mr. Calloran, with a sneer.

Aileen did not reply, and was about to leave the kitchen, when her steps were arrested with the words:

'I say, Ally!'

'Well, what is it now?' she asked.

'He has not jilted you, has he?'

'Who?'

'The chap as wrote that letter?'

'No.'

'It looks mighty like it,' soliloquized Mrs. Fermoy's first-born, when he found himself alone. ' Perhaps that is what has given her such a pain in her temper lately. I must ask Jack about this,' he decided, while Aileen went back to her shop in time to surprise Master Bertie, who had craftily taken advantage of the dialogue between his elders to slip out and fill his small cap and pocket with the fruit left momentarily at his mercy.

' He's been 'tealing your pears, Aunt Ally,' declared Minnie, who was herself in the act of descending from a raid in the window.

' Na—h, I warn't stealing yer pai—ars, I warn't stealing yer pai—ars !' shouted Bertie, in a wild fury; ' but her pinny is full of them.'

' I have only tooked one or two, and they was rotten,' whimpered the precocious young monkey, taking good care, however, not to display the contents of her apron.

' You are very bad children, both of you,' observed Aileen with conviction, personally conducting them into the street. ' Run away this minute, and don't let me see you here again, or I shall have something to say you

won't like. Be off now!' and she released
the small culprits, who, much relieved,
wended their way to a place they wot of
where such unholy gains as stolen pears,
'grabbed' pieces of loaf-sugar, and 'snatched'
cakes could be devoured in peace, the while
'Aunt Ally' returned to her accustomed seat
and re-read by the light of memory the letter
she had burnt.

It was from Philip Vernham, and ran
almost as follows :

'DEAR AILEEN,

'Mr. Desborne would like to see
you to-morrow, as near noon as may be
convenient. He assures me money will be
coming to you. Remembering what you
said six weeks back, I ventured to ask him
whether the amount would reach to fifty
pounds, and he answered, "Certainly ; to
considerably more."

'Yours faithfully,

'PHILIP VERNHAM.'

Here was something to think about—

something which had taken the colour out
of Aileen's cheeks, set her pulse fluttering
and her heart throbbing. More than fifty !
How much more, she wondered—perhaps a
hundred, perhaps two ; and then that jade
Fancy, who always delights in carrying those
who give heed to her far aloft, in order generally to drop them flat on the earth again,
whispered, 'Five hundred.'

'No, no,' argued Aileen's common-sense,
'it is impossible such a thing should be ; how
could my father's old uncle ever gather such a
fortune together ?'

'But,' persisted Fancy, jogging the girl's
memory, 'your father always told you how
"close and near" he was, how "beyond
clever" and "good at a bargain." He might
have put past five hundred pounds. Why,
even your father, who was not "close or
near," died leaving stock, goodwill, carts,
horses, and furniture, worth two hundred ;
you heard that said many a time.'

'Yes, indeed,' sighed Aileen ; 'and it went
like snow off a ditch.'

'So, you see,' said Fancy persuasively,

'quite probably five hundred pounds is coming to you, or *more*.'

'No,' answered Aileen to the tempter; 'it won't be five hundred or more; but it may stretch to a hundred, and if it should'—then she paused, and, after a minute, mentally added: 'I must take good care of it, and I will,' which utterance might be regarded as a solemn promise, sworn to on the New Testament, for, indeed, Aileen, though naturally generous, had found the necessity of keeping money, which, unless held well in hand, has a nasty habit of flying away and never coming back again.

'I must not sit here idle,' thought the girl, rising suddenly, 'or I shall lose my head. How it is going round! Will to-morrow never come that I may know?'

The morrow came—a day as fine, as bright, and as warm as that on which Mr. Philip's letter changed the aspect of life for Aileen.

'You'll be sure to look after the shop Mrs. Stengrove,' she said earnestly, as though no legacy had been looming in the near

future; and then, modestly attired in her
Sunday's best, she went tremblingly forth to
learn her fate.

When she reached Messrs. Desborne's
office, it was Mr. Puckle who answered her
timid inquiry with :

'Mr. Desborne is out, madam; but if you
walk upstairs Mr. Thomas Desborne is in,
and will attend to you. This way, please;'
and he went with her up that flight of stairs
Mr. Tripsdale had descended in such wrath.

CHAPTER XI.

WITH a strange sense that she was not Aileen Fermoy at all, but a greatly superior person, the girl walked into that office which was, so to speak, Messrs. Desborne's 'Board-room.'

Her unaccustomed feet sank deep into the Turkey carpet that covered the floor. Her eyes beheld with awe the huge, many-drawered table at which generation after generation of Desbornes had sat. She reverently surveyed the high mahogany 'nest.' containing tin boxes labelled with the names of honoured clients, and never asked herself how it was possible such crude ways of business could still obtain, ere, an inner door opening, she found herself confronted by a small spare man, who, after saying, with formal courtesy, 'I am glad to see you, Miss Fermoy,' placed a chair for her on one side of the great table, and, seating himself, took up his parable as follows :

· My nephew, whom you saw on the occasion of your previous visit, intended to be here to receive you. He must have been detained, however, and under the circumstances it is my privilege to communicate very good news to you.'

He paused, after the manner of a man accustomed to take snuff, and Aileen, thinking some answer was expected, said :

· Thank you, sir.'

· My nephew, I know, meant to say he feared you must have imagined we were very dilatory ; but the fact is, another claimant unexpectedly appeared in America. His pretensions, however, are satisfactorily disposed of, and it is therefore now, as I said, my privilege to inform you that you are the undoubted heiress to a very large fortune.'

' Yes, sir.' Then as Mr. Desborne did not

immediately **proceed**, she asked **diffidently,**
' To how much ?'

' To how much should you suppose ?' he
replied.

Aileen's **heart** beat wildly. **She** knew
from **Mr.** Thomas Desborne's **manner** the
amount must exceed fifty pounds by a good
deal, so she **almost** gasped out, marvelling at
her own temerity :

' Is it—is it, sir—two hundred ?'

The junior **partner** looked at her with a
sort of pitying wonder.

' When law costs have **been** paid—perhaps
you **may** have heard lawyers, unfortunately,
expect **to** be **paid**—there will be left for you,
as **nearly** as possible, *one hundred and thirty
thousand pounds !'*

' One **hundred** and thirty pounds, sir !'
said Aileen, **very** thankful, yet, it **must** be
confessed, somewhat disappointed.

' Thousand,' supplemented **Mr.** Thomas
Desborne.

' **What** is that, sir ?'

' Do you mean yearly income ?'

' I don't know what yearly income means, sir.'

'A yearly income,' explained Mr. Thomas Desborne, with that compassionate forbearance a right - minded man always evinces towards a woman's ignorance, ' means the amount, whether gained by labour or derived from the investment of capital, which a person has a reasonable right to depend upon receiving in the course of a twelvemonth. Your money, being remarkably well invested, will at the present time ensure you something over six thousand a year, or, roughly speaking, more than a hundred pounds a week.'

'But that can't be, sir. It's impossible !' said Aileen, not meaning, of course, that the gentleman was telling an untruth, but only that he must be utterly mistaken.

'Impossible or not, it is true,' was the answer.

'That I am to have a hundred pounds each week ?'

'Precisely.'

For a moment the girl looked at him with dilated eyes; then her lips parted, her gaze faltered, her head dropped, and, to Mr. Desborne's dismay, she burst into a passion of tears.

Here was a dilemma. In the whole course of his professional experience he had never found himself in so awkward a position.

He had, of course, seen women cry, but then he knew what they were crying about, and he could not form the faintest idea why this girl had covered her face with her hands and was weeping convulsively.

'What have I said? What have I done?' he exclaimed in despair, looking helplessly first at Aileen and then at the carafe with a vague intention of offering her a glass of water. 'This is really dreadful. I do wish Edward were here.'

As if in obedience to some incantation, at that instant the door opened and the Head of the Firm, looking pleasant and handsome as ever, came into the room with a light, buoyant step and a smile, which vanished at the sight of his uncle's horrified face and the sound of Aileen's unrestrained grief.

'I never was so glad to see you before,' said Mr. Thomas Desborne.

' Why, what is wrong ? What has happened ? Good heavens ! what is the matter ?'

' I cannot imagine ; I am completely in the dark. When I told Miss Fermoy the amount of her fortune, she broke down completely, and has remained in the state you see ever since.'

The elder man spoke as though Aileen had been weeping for a twelvemonth, and the younger naturally asked :

' Ever since how long has she been like that ?'

' I don't know ; it seems an immense time. Perhaps I was too abrupt, perhaps I ought to have led up to the subject more gradually, but who could have expected such an outbreak ? Can't you say something to her ?'

If his uncle had not known what to do, Mr. Edward Desborne proved equal to the occasion.

' My dear girl,' he began, laying a persuasive hand on her shoulder, ' do try to compose yourself. At least tell us what is troubling you so much. We are all friends here, and will help you if we can.'

It was strange to see the instantaneous

effect his voice had upon her. Making a desperate effort to check her sobs, Aileen lifted her eyes, swimming in tears, red and swollen with weeping, to his sympathetic face.

' Oh, sir,' she began, ' I'm———' But there she broke down again, and, burying her face in her handkerchief, cried hysterically.

' She will be better presently,' said Mr. Edward Desborne. ' Never mind us, Miss Fermoy ; let your grief, whatever its cause may be, have its way. We will leave her alone for a little,' he added in a low tone to his uncle, pointing to the inner room, which happened at that moment to be unoccupied.

' What do you suppose is the meaning of all this ?' asked Mr. Thomas Desborne.

' I can't tell ; but such a large windfall might well knock anyone over.'

' But it need not have made her cry,' said the elder man in an aggrieved tone. ' I never saw a woman cry in such a way before, and she did not say a word, but just began— and went on,' he added as an afterthought.

Mr. Edward Desborne laughed, and turned the subject by speaking of some matters which whiled away, perhaps, fifteen minutes, when a modest tapping at the door attracted his attention.

It was Aileen who, pale and shaken, but collected, stood on the threshold.

' I am ashamed of myself, sir,' she began. ' I can't think how it was I came to behave so foolishly. I am very sorry, and I hope you will excuse my taking the liberty of knocking, but I thought I would say I was going.'

' You must not go yet, if you please. There are many things we ought to speak to you about. If you remain quiet for a short time you will be able to talk. You shall have the office all to yourself.'

' Perhaps you would rather go upstairs, Miss Fermoy ?' suggested Mr. Thomas Desborne ; ' I think you will find my room more comfortable than an office. There are books you might like to look at.'

' An excellent thought,' chimed in the younger man. ' My uncle's sanctum is delightfully quiet, and you really must not go with those traces of tears still on your cheeks.'

'But I am giving so much trouble,' said the girl humbly.

'We hope you will give us much more trouble,' remarked the Head of the Firm with a smile. 'Shall I take Miss Fermoy upstairs, uncle?'

'No, I will do the honours of my City house,' answered the old lawyer, who felt puzzled how to adapt his formal code of courtesy to the needs of this strange client. 'This is my home,' he added, after they had ascended the next flight, ushering her into a room a little smaller and rather lower in the ceiling than that they had just left; 'and now you can remain quite undisturbed for hours if you like. This is a comfortable chair, and when you feel inclined to read, there is, as you see, enough of light literature to amuse you for an hour.'

'But, sir——'

'I must leave you now,' went on Mr. Thomas Desborne, unheeding this protest, 'but shall see you in an hour. Meantime, if you want anything, just touch that bell, and my housekeeper will answer it;' and he was gone before Aileen could utter another word.

With a strange sense of peace the girl sank back in the easy-chair the lawyer had wheeled round for her.

She was in sore need of peace and rest, and that seemed to her the very quietest room in the whole world; not a sound of the City traffic broke its silence. Double windows deadened all noise. Facing north, its atmosphere was cool and pleasant, especially as a ventilator deftly introduced into the wide old-fashioned chimney performed its intended work to admiration.

With tired eyes she looked around. There were bookcases which reminded her of the Rev. Mr. Vernham's study in the days gone by.

Poor Aileen! There was nothing gracious or good or tender her eyes saw, but recalled that far-away past when the Vernhams supplied all her soul lacked and heart desired.

That had been the best time of her life, when she trotted on little errands to the Curacy, and afterwards waited hand and foot on the 'dear lady,' Mr. Philip's mother; when Mr. Philip's cheery 'Good-morning, Aileen,' sounded pleasant in her ears, and Mrs. Vernham's 'Good-night, my dear child, and God bless you!' seemed sweet as the verse of a psalm.

Then it was she acquired that soft refinement of speech and manner which appeared strange in one so situated; then it was that by daily association with a gentlewoman—the most patient and loving of Christians—she began to discriminate, and learnt to know, a gentlewoman when she saw her, even when poorly clothed and stripped of adventitious surroundings.

And for this reason Mr. Thomas Desborne's bookshelves, though neither so wide nor high as those at the Curacy, recalled the memory of that gracious past, before sickness and death changed Aileen's home for the first time, and again sickness and death obliterated all save the memory of it.

But the girl could not forget, could never forget. Across the weary years of uncongenial work and unaccustomed hardship, tender hands seemed stretched forth to her in loving greeting.

There was a subtle scent in the room she remembered, but could not recognise, for it is not everyone who is familiarly acquainted with the faint yet pungent odour of Russia-leather.

Everything around her, even the stillness and peace of that strange room, so lonely amid thousands of people, so quiet within hearing of the roar of London, seemed like something given back.

Afterwards a soothing touch stilled her over-wrought nerves, gentle voices sounded in her ears, beautiful visions and pleasant thoughts came to her, for the girl slept.

Quite unawares, slumber overtook her, and brought visions of a lost paradise on its wings.

When had she known such a sleep ?

It was indeed an experience to thank God for most devoutly.

She awoke at last : not to a knowledge of where she was, but to a consciousness that someone was moving about the room.

'I hope I have not disturbed you, miss,' said that 'someone,' seeing the girl stir and push back her hair, which movement displaced a neat little bonnet. 'Mr. Desborne gave me particular orders not to waken you, and——'

'Have I been to sleep—here?' asked Aileen, horrified.

'You have had a beautiful sleep, miss, and I hope you are all the better for it. Mr. Desborne said as how he thought you might like a cup of tea, so I've kept a kettle boiling all the afternoon, and——'

'All the afternoon!' repeated Aileen ; 'why, what time is it now?'

'Just upon four o'clock, miss ; no, please don't stir. I'll fetch the tea, and then you'll feel better like knowing what you are doing.'

'Just upon four o'clock!' then she must have been fast asleep in Mr. Desborne's office for almost that number of hours. How could she have done such a thing? What would that gentleman think of her? And she pressed her cramped hands to cheeks that were painfully flushed, and wondered how she could ever make excuses and apologies enough.

For the girl was absolutely humble; in the innermost recesses of her heart there did not lurk one atom of self-esteem, and though Mr. Thomas Desborne had told her she was heiress to great wealth, that fact did not make her think more of Aileen Fermoy, or less of the 'gentlemen' through whom knowledge of her astounding good fortune had been conveyed.

'I thought, miss,' said the housekeeper, reappearing at this moment, 'it might refresh you just to bathe your face, so I have taken the liberty of bringing you some water;' and, spreading a snowy cloth over one of the small tables close at hand, she placed upon it a basin, which she filled from a great wide-mouthed ewer. Could it be for her—Aileen—who had not experienced one single womanly kindness since Death's hand fell heavily on her mother, that all this fuss was made? Could it be to Aileen Fermoy, who had gone from door to door asking those as poor as herself, 'Is there anything you want to-day, ma'am?' that this strange, unaccustomed courtesy was shown? Yes, it could be, and was; but, to her credit be it spoken, not then or ever did the girl say to herself, 'It is only because I am rich; they would not have been civil except for the money.' Could she have thought or said those things she would not have been the Aileen who, on that hot August afternoon, plunged her face into a basin of fair water, that indeed seemed to her the sweetest water in which woman ever laved.

'Thank you, thank you; you are so kind,' she said.

The housekeeper smiled. She did not understand the position of this young person at all, but it was enough for her that Mr. Thomas Desborne had wished every civility to be shown, even to the extent of that cup of tea for which a kettle had been kept in readiness for hours.

That tea was quite different from the strange concoction Mrs. Fermoy called by the same name, and, as the girl drank it eagerly, she thought how different everything was from what things had been when, earlier in the day, she tried to eat her breakfast and could not.

Just as she finished a slice of thin bread-and-butter, Mr. Edward Desborne came in.

' Better ?' he asked.   ' Oh, you look better. Now do you feel strong enough to discuss affairs, or would you rather leave matters over for a few days ?'

Very truthfully Aileen answered she would like to hear what he wished to say then and there, and accordingly, without further pre-amble, he repeated what his uncle had before mentioned.

' The money is safely invested,' he added, ' and we think you would do well to leave it where it is.'

' That must be as you think fit, sir, of course,' she replied.

' And about yourself.   As I have gathered, your home is not a comfortable one.   Will you think what you would like to do in the future, and tell us if we can help you in any way ?'

She did not answer him immediately ; she did not say she would think, because she was thinking deeply then.

' If this money is really coming to me, sir——' she began at last.

' Coming ! It has come ; it is yours.'

' I meant if it is not a dream, sir, from which I must waken soon, I should not care to go on as I am. Though there is no creature in the world belonging to me to care whether I am well-to-do or starving'—and her voice shook a little—' making a bad use of this fortune or spending it wisely, my father and mother would have cared, and I'd be glad to try and do what they would consider right— that is, if they could speak to me now, which they can't.'

' I understand ; it is a most admirable and natural feeling.'

' When the other gentleman told me such a mountain of money had come to me, I thought my heart would break, to remember there was nobody left to go home and tell such news to, nobody to be glad, nobody I could talk to and give to, and make plans with. It was like having a feast spread, with not a soul to sit down and eat but myself. That was what made me so foolish, and I hope you will forgive me.'

'Ah! you are not the only person who has experienced the same feeling,' answered Mr. Desborne. 'There was a man once who, after having lost parents, wife, children, won honours which made him the envy of his fellows. When congratulated, he only said, "Too late; there is no one left to care!" But life was behind that man, Miss Fermoy; life is before you to make a great and happy thing of in the future.'

'Yes, I feel that in a sort of way, which is why I'd be thankful if I could see what would be best for me to do—what would be right, I mean.'

'My wife is below; will you come down and speak to her? I am sure this is just a juncture at which her advice and opinion would be invaluable. I have been telling her about you, and she is deeply interested.'

Aileen hesitated and hung back, the colour coming and going in her cheeks, her pretty hair tossed a little about her forehead, her eyes soft with the deep tender look of one who had been gazing at a beautiful past through mists of sorrow.

'Do come!' he urged; 'my wife is the very person to put us all right.' But still the girl paused, reluctant to be so bold. 'You must not look on her as a stranger,' he went on; 'we are all your friends here, and a little sensible advice now may save a world of trouble hereafter.' The words were not much, but the way in which he spoke them proved irresistible. His cheery manner, his frank, pleasant voice, broke down the girl's scruples, and saying, 'Very well, sir, as you think it best,' she went with him into the large office where she had been told of her good fortune, and saw a gentle-woman who seemed to her the greatest lady in the land. She was not beautiful, but handsome, with a sort of statuesque state-liness which impressed everyone who saw her. As Aileen said afterwards, 'She is like a queen'; and certainly no queen who ever lived could have thought more of her-self and less of others than the Honourable Mrs. Desborne.

She was standing by the table, and turned as they entered.

'This is Miss Fermoy, Emily, of whom I was speaking just now,' explained her husband; and even at the dread moment it appeared strange to Aileen that he should venture to address such a vision by her Christian name.

'Oh, indeed!' said Mrs. Desborne, with a stately inclination of her head.

'And I have brought her to you for the benefit of a little counsel, which I know you will give.'

'If in my power, I shall be very happy, of course. What is it she wishes to consult me about?'

'Tell my wife exactly your difficulty; don't be nervous; explain to her what you would like.'

'Pray do,' added Mrs. Desborne. 'When I know the advice you stand in need of, I can give it so much better.'

'Then, if you please, ma'am,' said Aileen, half frightened by her own temerity, and rushing on as though in terror of breaking down midway, 'I'd like to learn how to be a lady——'

'Yes?' said Mrs. Desborne, with an enigmatical smile.

CHAPTER XII.

MISS SIMPSON.

WITH the quick instinct of her class, Aileen read that smile aright, and knew she had made a mistake.

'I don't mean a lady like you, ma'am; I know I never could be that. There are not many who could, even if they were well-born and well-bred; but just a plain sort of one, who would not be making mistakes and saying and doing wrong things ladies would never think of. I would try to give as little trouble and learn as fast as I could, if any person was so kind as to put me in the right way.'

'Yes,' said Mrs. Desborne again, but this time differently.

'In a common fashion, I am not so bad a scholar,' went on the girl eagerly. 'My

father was always anxious I should get learning, and Mrs. Vernham took a great deal of
pains to help me with my lessons. I can
write pretty well and cipher, and read almost
any word in a book; but I want to know how
to speak, and what to speak, and the way to
speak it.'

Words could not express the utter contempt
with which Mrs. Desborne heard this list of
Aileen's accomplishments; but she was not
offended, and said 'Yes' for the third time,
with a sort of compassionate toleration.

'I am convinced you would be a very apt
pupil,' remarked Mr. Desborne kindly.

'Indeed I would try hard, sir, to get on as
fast as I could.'

'I have no doubt of that,' said Mrs. Desborne; 'but I fear you fail to realize the
difficulties lying before you. At your age it
is not an easy matter to unlearn the habits of
years.'

If anything could have accentuated the
great truth contained in these words, that
accent was given by Mrs. Desborne's tone,
by Mrs. Desborne's manner.

Had she been a judge passing sentence of death on all Aileen's aspirations, she could not more pitilessly have conveyed her opinion that all efforts to become even a ' plain sort of lady ' were futile, and might as well be abandoned at once.

' But if I tried very hard, ma'am,' ventured the girl, daunted, but not quite crushed.

' You would succeed, I know,' said Mr. Desborne ; not because he knew in the least, but because it hurt him to see her look so disappointed.

' You do not quite understand, Edward,' said his wife with a little asperity ; ' even if it were possible to discover a school where such rudiments as Miss Fermoy requires to learn are included in the regular course—and I confess I never heard of such a school—she would find her position so painful as to be unendurable.'

' I should not like to go to school,' remarked Aileen.

' You hear ?' observed Mrs. Desborne, turning to her husband, with an air of calm superiority.

' No ; what I meant was, ma'am, that per-

haps some lady not very well off would teach
me what I want to know. If I could not learn,
I should not be much worse off than I am.'

'No,' said Mrs. Desborne doubtfully.

'I wonder whether an arrangement of that
sort would suit Mrs. Fletcher,' observed Mr.
Desborne.

'I do not know; you could ask, however,'
returned his wife, in a manner which implied
her opinion that Mrs. Fletcher's social standing was not much higher than the estimation
in which she held Aileen.

There ensued a pause, during the continuance of which no one spoke, and no one
seemed to have anything to suggest.

Mrs. Desborne's rich dress swept the floor,
and the room was filled by the scent of some
delicate perfume. Spite of the rebuff she had
received, Aileen's heart was filled with admiration, and she kept darting little glances of
awe and wonder at the lady Mr. Desborne
was so happy to call wife.

For all her averted eyes, Mrs. Desborne
caught many of these glances, and felt
gratified by Aileen's undisguised homage.

It seemed such a pity the girl had fallen into such a fortune! How much more fitting it would have been had Fortune seen fit to pour some of her favours into Mrs. Desborne's lap! But, alas! that could never be.

The Harlingfords' (her family) talents lay in the direction of spending—certainly not of saving—and someone must save if money is to be accumulated.

Suddenly a brilliant idea dispersed the gloom of Mr. Desborne's reflections and lighted up his face like a burst of sunshine.

' Did you not tell me a little time ago, my dear, that Miss Simpson said she should once again have to take a situation ?'

' Yes ; the foolish old thing invested her money in something which was to double her income, with the result that she has now lost nearly every penny.'

' Then Miss Simpson is the very person for us.'

' I do not think this is a thing which would suit her at all.'

' Don't you ? I really fancy it might.

She is such a dear lady, such a true gentlewoman. Yes, if Miss Simpson be still disengaged, the difficulty is solved.   I will write
to her at once.'

'It might be better that I should write, if
you really believe she ought to be written
to.'

'Which I certainly do,' he said, looking
happy as a schoolboy who has been given a
half-holiday.

'If she entertain the idea, she will require
very high terms.'

'Well, money is no object—is it, Miss
Fermoy?'

'I suppose not, sir; but I can't get used
to feeling I have any.'

'That state of mind will soon pass away.
—When will you write, Emily?'

'If the thing has to be done, I may as
well get it over at once,' answered Mrs.
Desborne in a tone of cold disapproval; 'but
I really do not think it is a charge Miss
Simpson would care to undertake.'

'Well, we can only put it to her, and she
can only refuse.   We might arrange a meet-

ing here.—What day would suit you, Miss Fermoy, to come into the City again ?'

'Any day, sir.'

'Any day is no day,' he answered with a smile. 'Please name one. Would Saturday or Monday be convenient ?'

'Monday, sir, would do very well.'

'Then, Emily, ask Miss Simpson if she could come here on Monday about three o'clock.'

'Shall I name a salary ?'

'Better not ; that can be settled afterwards. You might say, however, she will find pecuniary arrangements satisfactory.'

Mrs. Desborne sat down to write her letter, unwillingly, it is true, yet with a feeling that if the character of the Good Samaritan must be put on the stage, it was better she should play it. The 'old creature' would be very grateful, and she had always found Miss Simpson most useful.

'May I go now, sir ?' asked Aileen in a low voice, so as not to disturb the letter-writer. 'It is getting late, and it is a long way to Battersea.'

' I beg your pardon.   I ought not to have detained you; everything can wait till Monday.   You are certain you would rather not take any money now ?'

' Quite certain, sir.'

' I will see you downstairs,' said Mr. Desborne, holding the door open for her to pass out.

Aileen looked at Mrs. Desborne, not knowing whether to address that lady or not.

Just then Mrs. Desborne raised her eyes, and the girl took courage to speak.

' Good-afternoon, ma'am,' she said.

For answer, Mrs. Desborne inclined her head, after the manner of one acknowledging homage; and in another minute Aileen, having declined Mr. Desborne's offer to send for a cab, was walking towards Old Swan Pier like one in a dream.

She did not feel at all less dazed when she left the boat at Battersea, and bent her steps in the direction of a place she called home for want of a more suitable word.

CHAPTER XIII.

MR. THOMAS CALLORAN.

TEA was over when Aileen reached Field Prospect Road. On the oven a black teapot was standing stewing, into which Mrs. Fermoy immediately dashed a quantity of water, remarking, ' So you've come back at last, have you ?'

' Yes,' said the girl; ' I am very sorry to be so late, but I could not help it.'

' Then you'll have to help it, that is all I have got to say, and don't let me have to say it again. How do you think I am to keep a house over our heads without a penny of money to do it ? We have had no dinner to-day, and there were the poor little children crying fit to break their hearts with hunger. But much good it is talking to you about any-thing !'

'Had no dinner?' repeated Aileen, surprised. 'Surely our credit is not so bad you need have gone without dinner, even if I was out for once.'

'That is all you know about it. Do you think I was going to set my son down to boiled beef without a potato or a bit of greens, to say nothing of carrots, or, with plums just rolling about the place, to tell Tom his mother would not make him a pudding, when you know how fond he is of pudding, and him out of work, and desperate because he can't get any? No, I just told them one and all they would have to do without dinner, for that nasty, audacious woman had the impudence to tell me she was not going to let threepennyworth of anything go out of *your* shop, if you please, without the money. And as matters have come to this pass, I tell you straight you must choose between me and her, for I am not going to be insulted by such a come-of-nothing thing as that.'

'Very well,' sighed Aileen wearily.

'It's easy to say " very well," but before

all is said and done perhaps you'll find it very
ill. I am sick and tired of the whole business. When have I a minute to myself, or a
bit of pleasure like any other woman? It's
enough to make your poor father turn in his
grave to think of the way I am put upon.'

Aileen shuddered. Probably the words she
used did not mean much to Mrs. Fermoy, but
in the strained state of her nerves they
brought a fearful picture before the eyes of
Timothy Fermoy's daughter.

' I have tried to do my best,' she observed
humbly.

' Trying to do your best is one thing, and
doing it is another. If you had a grain of
respect for me, you'd never have left it in the
power of that woman to as good as say I was
a thief. Anyone might have thought myself
and the children were a gang of robbers. I'll
put up with it no more. Here for years and
years I have boarded, and lodged, and washed
you, and never asked for a penny-piece, and
this is the return I get.'

' But,' ventured Aileen, ' I have kept the
house.'

' Oh, I dare say !' scoffed Mrs. Fermoy, with a bitter laugh. ' So that's your last notion, is it ? What about Mr. Parkyn ? I suppose you mean I look on what he pays as pocket-money, as I might indeed, for hard I slave for it.'

' Would you mind speaking no more about the trouble ?' pleaded Aileen ; ' I have such a headache.'

' And do you think I have no headache ? Ay, I have, and a heartache, too ! If I had been pleasuring all day, as you have, I'd be ashamed to come home and talk as if nobody in the world had ever anything the matter with her but you. And I have not a half-penny to get some supper for Tom. Poor fellow ! he went out of the house like a raging lion when I told him he'd have to make shift with bread and cheese ;' and, to enhance the dramatic power of the picture herself had drawn, Mrs. Fermoy pointed an accusing finger towards the kitchen door, in order to strike Aileen dumb.

It seemed, indeed, to have this effect, for the girl rose from her chair and went out

without a word, returning in a minute or two
with a few shillings, which she laid as a sort
of peace-offering on the table.

'Now, never give me occasion to speak to
you again in the same way,' said Mrs.
Fermoy, swooping like an eagle down upon
the coins, and addressing Aileen as if she had
specially invited such vials of wrath to be
poured upon her head. 'I am going out to
get a crab for Tom. There is nothing he is
more partial to than crabs, and you might
pick out a good lettuce for him. I'm not
going into *your* shop again while that woman
is there;' having emphasized which dis-
tressing statement with a scornful toss of her
head, Mrs. Fermoy left the kitchen, leaving
Aileen to enjoy her tea with what appetite
she might.

The girl did not even try to enjoy it. She
went upstairs, changed her dress, washed up
the cups and saucers, put everything tidily in
its place, and then, going into the parlour for
coolness' sake, sat down wearily.

The morning's experience could not be
true. She felt at the time it was but a

dream, and now she knew it. She had always expected to awake suddenly, and what a shock the awakening seemed !

Was this, indeed, to be her life for ever ? Such a life ! And she clasped her hands across her throbbing forehead, and thought, as she had often and often thought before, ' I cannot bear it any longer—I *cannot !'*

But, after all, were Mr. Desborne's words a dream ? Had he not said them ? Would he have spoken them if untrue ? Was she going crazy ? Had she only imagined she went down the river and walked into the City and up the staircase in Cloak Lane ? Was Mr. Philip's letter a delusion ? She did not know, and she had nothing tangible by means of which she might tell whether recent events were the offspring of delirium or the legitimate children of fact.

Then, as her tired memory went back a little further, she knew there was one way in which she might ascertain the truth.

It had been no fancy dream that Dick stole her money, and surely no dream that Mr.

Desborne lent her the amount needful to make up her loss.

'Mrs. Stengrove,' she said, entering the shed where that 'come-from-nothing' woman was resting for a minute from her labours, 'I am so tired this evening, and my head is aching so much, I can't remember quite clearly; but did I not last Whit Tuesday ask you to take care of five pounds for me?'

'You did—five gold sovereigns, new from the mint. It was the first money you ever brought to me.'

'Thank you,' answered the girl; 'that is all I wanted to know.'

'You took it away next market morning.'

'Yes, I recollect now. I could not be quite sure;' and the girl stood silent, while a slow sense of relief surged through her heart. After all, it might be, then, that the impossible was the possible!

And if it were, oh! if it were, what was she to do next?

'Mrs. Fermoy has been going on awful,' said that ill-used woman's *bête noire* in a voice so awe-stricken as to indicate the tempest had been severe. 'She called me all the names she could lay tongue to, because I would not let her have her choice of the shop, and flew out like a mad-woman when I told those young imps of Tom Calloran's to keep their hands from picking and stealing.'

'I know,' answered Aileen, still trying to realize the fortune she had been told of might not prove to be a myth.

'Ay. I suppose she has been giving it to you, too. I can't make her out at all. She's ten times worse than she used to be. She went on to-day more like a mad-woman than anything else. If she drank, now, I could understand her, but——' she added tentatively.

'She does not,' was the decided answer. 'The trouble is that she lets her temper run away with her every now and then. Tempers are like horses, I suppose—they need to be bridled.'

'Hers, I should think, would need to be bitted and curbed as well,' finished Mrs. Stengrove, with a sharp bitterness which proved how severe had been the encounter. 'Once

or twice I really thought she was going to
strike me, and if she had I tell you straight
I'd have called the police. If you like to
stand her, I don't think other people ought.'

'Try, Mrs. Stengrove,' entreated Aileen,
'do try to be patient as you have been for a
while longer.' She was going to add, 'It will
only be for a short time,' but some inexpli-
cable dread of rashly challenging Fortune
stayed the words on her lips.

'Since you ask me,' answered the other,
'I will try, for you have been past the
common kind to us. I don't know how we
ever could have got through our trouble without your help; but Mrs. Fermoy is dreadful.
Sometimes it seems to me she is beyond bearing.'

'Perhaps if you had as many unruly
boys——' began Aileen, still bent on being
apologetic.

'But that's just what I would not have,'
interrupted Mrs. Stengrove. 'Whose fault is
it that her boys are so unruly? Why, hers,
and no other person's. No one can say I am
not a kind mother, but when I tell my young

ones a thing is to be done, it has to be done.'

Aileen did not answer. She felt too tired either to agree or to disagree, and though in a vague sort of way it occurred to her Mrs. Stengrove's children were by nature very different from the wild, headstrong Callorans, she knew nothing about ' heredity,' and while she firmly believed in original sin, she could not have talked learnedly concerning either if her life had depended on doing so.

There must always be those who feel rather than speak ; whose thoughts, incapable of being expressed verbally, find visible utterance in deeds which He who knows the heart wots of, though man forgets to notice, frequently only because his attention is not called to them.

For some reason unknown to her, yet still sufficient, Aileen knew there were excuses for all the Callorans, mother included ; they could not, as the Irish phrase goes, ' help the blood in them '—and who indeed, save by the grace of God, may cast out the ' black drop ?' —wherefore, even when she was most downhearted herself, she did not feel inclined to sit in judgment on them.

Only she was weary of it all—weary, physically and mentally, beyond the power of human expression. There was a strong feeling on her that evening that she would like to do the right thing; that though her head ached as it had never ached before, and her limbs were weary from that nervous exhaustion which fortunately spares, as a rule, those who earn their living in the sweat of their brow, it would be right and seemly to go not merely one mile, but two, along a disagreeable road, to answer Mrs. Fermoy's ungracious demands graciously, and to make life as pleasant as she could for her father's widow.

It was not much she could do *then*, but that little she did. She selected three of the finest lettuces and carried them indoors; afterwards she returned and filled a bushel basket with the vegetables Mrs. Fermoy's heart yearned after, Mrs. Stengrove looking on wonderingly.

'Where is Jack?' Aileen asked when all this was done.

'I gave him a shilling to get his tea,' answered the other. 'I knew you would not mind, and he said there was no peace in-doors.'

Aileen sighed; she could not controvert the statement. Was it not one she had made herself in quite cool blood in a tone of utter conviction to Mr. Philip?

'When he comes back,' she answered, 'will you ask him to bring these things in, and then you can go; he will see to the shop.'

'But what is all this?' exclaimed Mrs. Stengrove, into whose hand Aileen had pressed some money. 'You don't know what you are giving me.'

'I do,' said the girl; 'you have been worth that to me.'

'Are you sure you're well?' asked the woman, who really thought Aileen must be a little 'off her head.'

'No, I am not well,' was the answer; 'but I shall be to-morrow.'

'Then there's three shillings of her money till she is well,' said Mrs. Stengrove to her husband, placing that amount in coins of the realm under a china shepherdess on the mantelpiece. 'I am not a-going to impose on her, let other people do as they like.'

'She's a grand girl, that Aileen Fermoy,' replied the poor pale man, who was gradually getting better.

'She is, and she shan't be put upon if I can help it,' was the reply.

For there is a loyalty among the poor as often to be met with as honour among their betters. Generally it savours more of personal feeling than of abstract principle. When the uneducated are loyal, it is because they love some individual or hate some other; the rich, when honourable, are so to friend and foe alike. It is an impartial sentiment which impels a man to do right for the mere sake of right-doing, and is therefore far more satisfactory, and much more to be depended upon, than any action prompted by mere passion.

Nevertheless, the loyalty of the poor serves a very good purpose indeed, and produces often most excellent results, as, for example, when it prompted Mrs. Stengrove to protect

Aileen from the consequences of her own generosity.

'The girl is so worried she does not know what she is doing,' thought the matron, and she therefore tucked three shillings out of five carefully away under the smiling shepherdess, who had in a similar manner protected many an odd threepence and sixpence.

Aileen in her time had tried similar hiding-places with disastrous results. There was no spot the ingenuity of woman could think of that the misdirected cleverness of boyhood failed to discover; but the Calloran youths were older in years and sin than the Stengroves, and what seemed to the first mere diversion would have appeared to the last one step to the scaffold!

It was quite late before Mrs. Fermoy came back, tired but in high good humour. She had been to the Wandsworth Road for her crab, and returned with four instead of one, having secured that number for threepence less than she was asked in Battersea, or, rather, than she had 'beat down' the Battersea vendor to.

True, she spent two-thirds of her savings in travelling, and hours of time besides; but, then, her time was not of much value to herself or any other person, and she had ample value for her tram-fare in the pleasure she derived from making a chance acquaintance to whom she confided the story of her many troubles, including how she had buried two husbands and four children, and been forced to struggle with the world, a thing she never expected to have to do, and that her father and mother never expected she would have to do, either, for 'they lived private and were much respected;' how she had four boys still living, and 'good boys, too, thank God;' how she had to make a home for her eldest son, who was a widow man: his wife fell into a decline, poor soul! after the birth of her second child, and 'dear children they are, and pretty, as you would say if you saw them;' how she, the speaker, was better than a mother to the orphans, bringing them up to mind what their elders told them; how she had a sore handful with her second husband, nursing him day and night, often never taking her clothes off for weeks together, and spending pounds and pounds in buying things he never touched ; how she had been left badly off, and did not know what would have become of them all if she had spared herself, as too many women do, and not buckled to work and slaved worse than any West Indian, as she might say ; how she had a step-daughter who, instead of being the comfort she ought to be, was very trying, having a great opinion of herself, as her father before her had of himself, and ' people like that never think much of anybody else ; no, you might lie down under their feet and let them tramp over you and they'd never say " Thank you :" some are like that !' And doubtless she would have added much more to the same effect, embellished with many ingenious flights of fancy, had not the conductor, putting in his head and saying ' Now, ma'am,' spirited her companion away.

' Has not Tom come home yet ?' she asked, looking with satisfaction at the supper-table, on which Aileen was placing the crabs she had scientifically dissected and prettily arranged with parsley decorations.

'I have not seen him,' answered the girl ;
' but Jack and Peter are outside.'

' Then you had better call them. I feel
just famished. I did not think I could touch
a morsel when I went out, but there is
nothing like a blow to give a body an
appetite ; and, Ally, you might just send
Jack to the Bedford Arms for a pot of six
ale. Tom is sure to be back for his share
of that. Oh, and we'll need vinegar, dear,
and I think there is nothing else.'

Aileen sent and paid for the pot of ale ;
she brought in the vinegar ; she hunted up
Bertie and Minnie, who had fallen asleep
beside the fence ; and then she took her seat
on a low stool away from the fire and the
light.

' Aren't you going to have some supper ?'
inquired Mrs. Fermoy.

' I am not hungry, thank you,' said Aileen.

' There you go,' was the reply, ' wasting
good victuals, and then making out you're not
strong !'

' Not strong !' repeated Aileen with a
laugh ; ' when did I ever say I wasn't strong ?'

'If you did not, somebody else did for you,' was the vicious retort; 'and more shame for them, since by comparison an elephant is weakness itself. If you were like me, now, with that awful pain in my side, and that wind gathering round my heart, and the awful ache in my back that bends me double every now and again, you'd have something to complain of.'

'Indeed,' answered the girl very earnestly, 'I do not complain. What is there for me to complain about? I am as well as anyone need wish to be. I only wish I could cure that pain in your side and back. Won't you go to the doctor and ask him if he can't give you something?'

'No; I won't. It is all very fine for you, who make your own money and take good care to keep it, going to doctors; but if I wasted the little I make as you do, I wonder what would become of us all.'

Mrs. Fermoy's was a profound conundrum, and Aileen did not attempt to answer it; she only knitted on in silence, while Mrs. Fermoy, after surveying the crab, the vinegar, the beer, and the other adjuncts, remarked, 'It don't seem much good waiting for Tom,' fell to herself, and invited Jack and Peter to follow.

And not merely Jack and Peter, but those 'blessed darlings' Bertie and Minnie, who had many special morsels, and a few sips from the friendly tankard, which was drained by Mrs. Fermoy and family, and again replenished, before Mr. Calloran, full of beer and anger against society as at present constituted, returned very drunk to give his family the doubtful advantage of his companionship. Between him and his mother, it is scarcely necessary to say, there immediately ensued a most frightful quarrel. Naturally, she felt aggrieved that, after having 'demeaned herself' so far as to ask Aileen for money, and gone all the way to the Wandsworth Road 'beating down crabs when she was so tired she did not know how to put one foot before the other,' Tom should not merely decline to partake of supper, but stigmatize the food provided as 'stinking stuff'; still, it may be doubted whether she was quite wise to answer his discourteous observation in kind.

This was what she did, however—what, moreover, she was in the habit of doing. One word led to more. It is always a rash experiment to reproach a man who has not a penny in his pocket, and who knows he has spent his last penny foolishly. Mr. Calloran was too drunk to consider the nature of his remarks, and Mrs. Fermoy might quite as well have been drunk, because she lost all self-control as utterly as though she had been standing at the bar of the Bedford Arms for a whole day, treating and being treated. Tom said whether he was in work or out of it she never gave him a meal fit to put before a pig, whereupon Mrs. Fermoy said a pig would have more manners than he—that he was a lazy, useless, ungrateful, drunken hound, who had no more spirit than a dog, or he would not eat his widowed mother out of house and home, and bring his two children to help eat her out of it too. Whereupon Tom retorted thickly:

'I am d——d well sick of this, and for

two pins would take my hook this minute and never come back again.'

'Why don't you take your hook, then?' jeered Mrs. Fermoy; 'who's keeping you? who wants you to stop? If it is me you are thinking of, I don't.'

'Then just for that very reason I'll stay.' replied Mr. Calloran, who had sense enough left to remember that if he banged his mother's door behind him there was no other likely to fly open at his approach. 'I have always paid you for my keep handsome when I was in work, and now I am out of it you may keep me for a variety.'

'You are a nice sort of a fellow, you are!' screamed Mrs. Fermoy, in a paroxysm of rage; 'call yourself a man and live on a woman! But there must come an end to it. I have borne with you too long, and I'll bear with you no longer. Out you go to-morrow before twelve o'clock, mind. You'll get no more dinners from me. I have been a good mother to you, and this is my reward; this is what any mother may expect that——'

The world was never destined to hear the end of Mrs. Fermoy's declamation, for it was cut short by the sounds of a piercing scream, a fall and howls, which proceeded from the end of the table, which Minnie, under cover of the domestic storm, had mounted with a view of possessing herself of some further portions of crab.

Bertie, perceiving her design, and virtuously bent on frustrating it, instantly proceeded to seize a choice morsel she had just annexed, with the result that Minnie tumbled on the floor with a frantic yell, pulling Bertie after her by his hair.

Anyone might have supposed the end of all things earthly had arrived ; the crash of kingdoms, the horrified lamentations of doomed millions, could hardly have made more noise than those two wretched little children rolling on the ground, kicking, beating, and biting each other, managed to produce. To add to the din, Mrs. Fermoy began scolding the juvenile sinners at the top of her voice, while Mr. Calloran inquired, in a deep bass, the quality of which was somewhat impaired by beer: 'Why are not those little devils in bed ?'

Aileen made no reply. Shaking in every limb, for the family amenities always terrified the girl, she tried to separate the combatants, but was pushed aside by Mrs. Fermoy who, exclaiming, 'A fine lot of use you are !' jerked Bertie, yelling with pain and rage, to his feet, and administering two sounding blows, one on the right side of his head and another on the left, sent him reeling across the room, and then turned her attention to that 'cunning image, the artfullest young jade in Battersea,' Minnie.

'Here, you keep your hands off my children !' exclaimed Mr. Calloran, rising in wrath and vainly trying to steady himself; ' if you do not, I'll——' At which point, staggering ignominiously, he fell back into his chair, from which safe ground he glared at his mother with much ferocity.

'Oh, do be quiet !' entreated Aileen, addressing both the combatants; 'we shall have the neighbours in soon if you go on in this way. I'll take Minnie.—Run upstairs.

Bertie, and stop crying. Had not you better get to bed ?' she added, speaking to Mrs. Fermoy; 'Tom can have his sleep out here.'

'I'll go to bed when I think fit,' returned Mrs. Fermoy, with great dignity; 'and as for Tom, I won't have drunken brutes sleeping in my kitchen.'

The person thus described rose once more, this time to hurl part of a loaf at his parent.

He missed his aim, however, though the target was a large one, and at the same moment, tripping over a piece of carpet which had been displaced during the children's fray, he fell full length on the floor, bruising himself terribly.

The noise brought Jack and Peter, who had gone to their room some time before, downstairs again, only half awake.

'What is the row ?' they both asked in a breath; 'anybody killed ?'

But Tom neither moved nor spoke; the fall had stunned him.

'He's dead! I'm sure he is!' screamed Mrs. Fermoy. 'I always knew this would be the end of it.'

With great exertion the lads turned their brother over. Aileen ran for water and sprinkled some upon Mr. Calloran's face, while Mrs. Fermoy sat rocking herself and sobbing hysterically.

Then there ensued a comparative silence, more dreadful than the storm which had preceded it, during which even Bertie and Minnie stinted their crying, and the rest looked questioningly at each other.

' Do you think——' began Aileen with white cheeks and chattering teeth.

At that moment Tom opened his eyes and a drop of water trickled into one of them.

' What the —— are you up to ?' he feebly muttered.

' Come, he's worth a dozen dead uns !' said Peter in a tone of cheerful relief. ' He'll be right as ninepence presently; he's only shaken a bit.'

CHAPTER XIV.

CERTAINTY.

It was a dreadful house from which Aileen, in very bad spirits, went out on the Monday following, to keep her appointment in Cloak Lane. She had been to market in the morning, and returned to find Tom, who was laid up with the injuries received on crab-supper night, still bemoaning himself in bed, with a bottle full of doctor's stuff on a table by his side for company.

As usual, the children were disporting and quarrelling on the pavement ; as usual, Mrs. Fermoy was gossiping, and also as usual, the thermometer of her temper rose to blood-heat when she beheld her stepdaughter going forth 'dressed up like a lady, to take your pleasure as if you were one.'

' I am going out on business,' was the answer.

' Oh, indeed ! It would seem as if business away from Battersea has much increased of late.'

' It has,' replied Aileen, walking off without another word.

Anyone who looked more unlike a girl to whom had come news of a fortune than Aileen, as she stepped on board the steamboat, it would be difficult to conceive. Rather, with her pale cheeks and anxious eyes, she resembled a person who sees a heap of fairy gold change into withered leaves.

In a vague, desponding way she thought, as the vessel glided on, of the pennies she had squandered in going up and down the river, led by that will-o'-the-wisp advertisement ; of the hours she had wasted ; of the hopes in which she had permitted herself to indulge ; of the waking dreams from which loud voices and angry words had brought her back to the realities of a struggling existence, unillumined by love, uncheered by kindness.

Aileen felt very sorry, not exactly for herself, perhaps, but for the foolish girl who had let imagination run away with her. Indeed, she felt so sorry while recalling the illusions of that golden summer, which seemed to her now like the incidents in some pretty, sad story-book, she was only roused from her reverie by the bumping of the vessel against Old Swan Pier and a general exodus across the gangway.

'By your leave, miss,' said a boatman, who was manœuvring a thick rope close by where Aileen sat.

'I beg your pardon,' she answered, perceiving she was in the way, and then she, too, followed the crowd ashore, and bent her steps up Swan Lane into Thames Street.

In the after-days, still all to come, she trod those same stones with an even sadder heart; but that was the last time she ever wended her way through the City feeling utterly poor and desolate. For Shawn Fermoy's wealth was fact, and the fortune to which Timothy Fermoy's daughter had succeeded no phantom !

On that occasion it fell out quite accidentally that Mr. Knevitt was in the outer office when Messrs. Desborne's new client entered.

From Mr. Puckle he had received a circumstantial report of Aileen's dress and appearance on the occasion of her first visit, and with that deeply impressed on his mind, it was natural, perhaps, even so astute an individual as the managing clerk should fail to recognise in a girl dressed like thousands of other working girls, only a little more quietly, the 'costeress' who so startled the proprieties of Cloak Lane at Whitsuntide.

Mr. Knevitt was lounging on the hearth, leaning back against the mantelpiece, awaiting Mr. Tripsdale's return from an errand on which he had sent him, and reluctantly turned his head a little in order to answer Aileen's modest enquiry.

'Is Mr. Desborne in ?'

'He is engaged,' was the curt answer.

The girl paused and hesitated. Could this be the beginning of the end ? Then she remembered how she had been rebuffed more than three months previously, and her courage revived.

'If you please,' she began in her pretty way, not adding 'sir,' however.

Somehow she did not feel inclined to do such honour to Mr. Knevitt.

'It is not of the slightest use,' he replied brusquely ; 'Mr. Desborne is particularly engaged and must not be disturbed. You can leave any message with me.'

It was all very like her former experience, with a difference—so like, that Aileen could scarcely forbear smiling.

'But Mr. Desborne told me to come back to-day about three o'clock,' she said, speaking quickly, in order to prevent another interruption.

Mr. Knevitt this time altogether removed his shoulder from contact with the chimney-piece, and, assuming a more businesslike attitude, asked to be 'favoured with her name.'

'Fermoy,' answered the girl.

'I must beg to apologize,' said Mr. Knevitt in some confusion ; 'but I did not know—I thought,' he added dexterously, 'it was an older lady Mr. Desborne expected. I am very sorry. Perhaps you will walk into the office and take a seat, while I inform Mr. Desborne of your arrival.'

Aileen accepted the chair he placed for her, and looked round the room where her first interview had taken place in much better spirits. She was not deficient in worldly wisdom, and knew very well the sudden alteration in Mr. Knevitt's manner must have been produced by a belief that Aileen Fermoy was a girl worth being civil to.

Not Aileen Fermoy herself, she thoroughly understood ; but Timothy Fermoy's daughter, Shawn Fermoy's heiress. And for this reason she went on to argue there must be some truth in the story about her wonderful fortune. Everybody could not be mistaken, certainly not that determined-looking, off-hand-spoken clerk.

Just as she arrived at this conclusion, she heard someone running quickly downstairs, and the next moment Mr. Desborne opened the door.

' Ah ! Miss Fermoy,' he exclaimed, ' I am

glad you have come. Miss Simpson is upstairs, and I think everything is right.   If
you put on your prettiest manners, and speak
to her in your nicest way, I am sure everything will be right.   She is the dearest
creature, but at first she may strike you as a
little formal. You must not mind that, however.'

Aileen's heart sank within her.   To be
told even laughingly that it was necessary to
put on her prettiest manners, and speak in
her nicest way, did not sound at all promising, but yet the first sight of Miss Simpson
rather tended to dispel her fears.   She was a
lady, not of uncertain age, but of an age
perfectly apparent to the most casual observer.
She must have been a pretty young woman ;
indeed, she was a pretty old one, with her
brown hair plentifully mixed with gray,
braided smoothly on her forehead, and that
delicate pink-and-white complexion which is
now so rarely to be seen.   She had truthful,
clear, kindly, dark-blue eyes, and her face
wore an expression in which shrewdness and
simplicity were curiously mingled.   For the
rest she was of middle height, well dressed,

and looked a gentlewoman from the crown of her head to the hem of her garment.

' Allow me to introduce Miss Fermoy to you, Miss Simpson,' Mr. Desborne said, a little nervously.

' How are you, Miss Fermoy?' added Mr. Thomas Desborne, greeting the shrinking girl with hearty kindness. ' This is Miss Simpson, whom to know is to esteem.'

Miss Simpson bent her head in acknowledgment of the introduction and compliment. As she did so, at one glance she took in the girl's whole appearance, which apparently proved satisfactory, for she put out her hand, and observing, ' I am sure we shall be friends,' won Aileen's heart instantly.

' Indeed, ma'am, I'd be very grateful,' she answered, in the soft, low voice rough work and rude association had not been able to make coarse.

Then there ensued a pause, during which no one seemed exactly to know what to say— a pause that might have proved awkward had Mr. Thomas Desborne not come again to the rescue.

'You would like to have a quiet talk together,' he remarked, addressing Miss Simpson. 'You will come to an understanding much sooner without our help. Good-bye for the present. I am so glad to have seen you again. For the sake of all parties concerned,' he went on significantly, 'I hope my nephew will be able to tell me an entirely satisfactory arrangement has been come to.—Edward, I want a word with you before I go out.—Good-afternoon, Miss Fermoy;' and, having made his old-fashioned farewells, the junior partner left the office, followed by the Head of the Firm.

CHAPTER XV.

'You heard the objection Miss Simpson made about undertaking this charge,' began Mr. Thomas Desborne, when he and his nephew were seated in the lower room, Mr. Knevitt still keeping solitary watch and ward in the clerks' office.

'Yes, but it is not insuperable. After all, the whole affair cannot but be regarded as a mere matter of money, of which, as Miss Fermoy has plenty, and poor Miss Simpson practically none, there ought not to prove much difficulty in arranging details so as to suit them both. It is really a splendid chance for our old friend, and her companionship would be of the greatest advantage to our new client.'

'Has it ever occurred to you, Ned, in any arrangement which is completed there are others besides Misses Simpson and Fermoy whose prosperity might be taken into account?'

'No, certainly not. Whose?'

Mr. Edward Desborne asked this question curiously. It was evident he had not the faintest idea what his uncle really meant, though there was a certain uneasiness in his manner which indicated a doubt as to whether something unpleasant might not underlie the suggestion.

Mr. Thomas Desborne did not instantly reply. He sat for a few moments with his head bent, tapping the table softly with the tips of his fingers.

'Whose prosperity?' repeated Mr. Edward Desborne a little impatiently.

'Ours,' answered the elder man, lifting his head and looking straight into eyes that wavered and shrank a little under his searching gaze. 'Ned, I hate going over all the old ground, but I cannot help myself. Our prosperity ought to be taken into account. The

interests of this firm should for once be considered. Suppose you try to remember it
is no sin for charity to begin at home, though
I admit charity ought not to end there.'

' Why, what have I done now ?' inquired
his nephew. ' What have I failed to do ? No
man ever worked harder over any troublesome
business than I to bring this Fermoy complication to a satisfactory conclusion.'

' No man can work harder or better than
you, Ned, when you choose. I only wish you
would devote as much time and energy to
other cases as you have done to this Fermoy
affair.'

' I fancied it was in something connected
with the Fermoy affair you thought I had
failed.'

' No, but I think you are going to fail.'

' How—in what way ?'

' In letting it slip out of your fingers.'

' I do not understand what you mean.
Pray speak more plainly.'

' I am going to do so. You can't deny that
for years our income has been decreasing.'

' Many incomes have been decreasing ; but

let us say, in order to simplify matters, that
ours is the only one in such case. What
then ?'

'Why, then it might be prudent to face
facts—to ask why it has decreased, and to
take measures to prevent any further diminu-
tion in the future.'

'You have often mentioned the causes
which you suppose have operated against our
success,' said the Head of the Firm coldly.

'If we are to maintain even our present
position, I must mention again the causes
which I *know* have reduced one of the finest
legal businesses in the City to the level of a
fourth-rate one,' was the reply.

Mr. Desborne made no comment ; he had
none to make ; facts are facts, let them be as
unpleasant as they will, and if his uncle were
determined to review them, it was hopeless to
try to prevent his doing so. For this reason
he only moved his position a little, and waited
with an outward semblance of patience which
ill concealed the annoyance he felt.

'The first mistake we made,' began Mr.
Thomas Desborne, speaking not for self and

nephew, but for many a Desborne dead and gone, snugly tucked up in vaults under old City churches, or, more recently, buried with considerable pomp and a good deal of expense in Abney Park and Highgate Cemeteries, ' was in starting such a ridiculous theory as that the eldest son of the eldest son, no matter how young, foolish, or inexperienced, was the only fit person to represent the firm. Older men, wiser men, more capable men, might be his prime ministers, his generals, his advisers, but were never permitted to rule with the head, and this merely because the founder of our business chanced to be a man in a thousand, astute, clever, incorruptible—a worthy descendant of an old race.'

' My dear uncle, pardon me for a moment, but is it necessary to go over all this again ? I quite agree with you that the whole arrangement was a mistake from the very first. It is a mistake now. Let us, as I have often before suggested, change places. Take the whole conduct of the business. I will be junior partner ; tell me what you wish done, and I will try to do it.'

'Will you indeed, Ned?' asked his uncle sadly. 'If so, it does not matter by what name you are called, or what your real standing in the firm chances to be. Were I the head of the Desbornes, and you my son, I could not have your interests more at heart, or sacrifice my own pleasure and comfort more than is the case. I have not, like others of the family, taken my money, my time, my energies, such talents as God has seen fit to give me, out of the business in order to found or join an opposition firm. If from the first the Desbornes had worked with, not against, each other; if those of the family who possessed special abilities had been assigned posts as chiefs of different departments, what might we not have been now? Why, the first firm of lawyers in the kingdom, instead of a decaying "house."'

He paused, but no answer came. What could his nephew say? What could anyone say who, recalling the past, contemplated the present?

The Desbornes had not resembled the typical bundle of sticks; rather, one by one, the

younger members had gone out alone into the
world, with the result that where any success
had been compassed the old name was
swallowed up among those of more adaptable,
though not more honourable, men. For
from the first the Desbornes had prided themselves not merely upon their honesty, but
their honour. Their traditions were founded
upon those of that good time when a City
merchant was a man who stood before the
world *sans peur et sans reproche*. Their businesses, their professions, were as dear and
valuable to them as empires are to kings.
Merchants first, they stood high amongst
those who helped to make London City the
power it was and is, and when one of the
family, the only one destined to convey the
name down to modern times, chose for his
career law instead of commerce, he took with
him to the Courts no less a probity than dis-
tinguished his relations on 'Change.

Small wonder Thomas Desborne felt proud
of the race from which he sprang.

In the Desborne annals there was to be found
no record of traitor, profligate, or spendthrift.

'Loyal and true' might have been the family motto, so well did they act up to its spirit. Loyal and true were the men who sat facing each other on that August afternoon, but one of them had a flaw of which no Desborne in the former time could have been accused. He was weak. His armour was not thrice plated, like that of his ancestor, the soldier citizen, who donned it for the sake of God, king, and country.

'But it is of little use talking of what has been,' resumed the elder man, at length. 'All we can do, all I desire to do, is to strive to keep the little which is left to us.'

'That surely we ought to be able to manage,' said his nephew, brightening up at once. An optimist by nature, he could never endure to hear unpleasant things mentioned. When out of sight they were with him out of mind; when hidden away they were to all intents and purposes non-existent. 'As I gathered, you intended a few minutes ago to mention something I had neglected or overlooked in connection with Miss Fermoy's matter. What is it, uncle? Do not be afraid of annoying me. I am a careless fellow, I know.'

'You are only careless, Ned, as regards your—or rather our—interests. When you undertake another man's business, you carry it through better than I could myself; and if we manage matters as it seems to me we may, Miss Fermoy is certain to turn out a valuable client.'

'I am sure of that; she will always be wanting our help in some way.'

'She will always be wanting the help of someone,' amended his uncle. 'The question is whether that help shall be given by us or another.'

'I fail quite to comprehend——'

'I will explain. We are now close to where the roads part. Shall Miss Fermoy continue to travel with us, or shall we allow her to drift away, and so lose *her* business and her money?'

'What makes you ask such a question? Of course she will stay with us. We can't afford to lose the management of her affairs.'

'Precisely what I think; but consider,

Ned, how many clients have already left us we could so ill afford to lose.'

' Is that my fault ?'

' I am afraid so. I see men come here every day who want subscriptions, or your name, or your time, or your assistance in some direction ; but what I do *not* see is that they bring or send any profitable business to us. On the other hand, I do notice that when any profitable business is attached to charitable projects other firms reap the advantage. Men praise you, Ned, but it is possible to pay too high for praise.'

' I never did anything for the sake of praise,' said Mr. Desborne indignantly. ' Uncle, do me justice. In anything I have tried to do for my fellow-creatures no thought of praise or profit has influenced me. With no consent of mine is my name connected with any good work. It is enough for me to see the work is done, to know the poor have been helped, the hungry fed, the sorrowful comforted.'

' I believe you,' answered Mr. Thomas Desborne ; ' but the result is as disastrous as though you had sought to be known for a philanthropist. While good works are going on, the poor helped, the hungry fed, the sorrowful comforted, we are being ruined. People say, and say rightly, that a man cannot do two things well. It is impossible for him to cure all the ills flesh is heir to and attend to his clients at one and the same time. City folks are cautious folks, and though they like you, they prefer to take their business to a lawyer who has time to devote to it, and not to one whose name appears more frequently in the reports of charitable societies and in the columns of fashionable papers than in matters connected with the law courts and his own profession.'

Edward Desborne flushed scarlet.

' You hit very hard,' he said.

' If I saw a man about to fall over a precipice, I should not wait to put on gloves before clutching him.'

' And do you think I am falling over a precipice ?'

' I think it behoves you to look where you are going.'

They sat for awhile without speaking a word. Then Edward Desborne remarked:

'I know you did not mean to vex me, uncle, but it would be idle to deny your accusation holds a cruel sting. Let that pass, however. This unhappy conversation had its origin in something connected with the Fermoy legacy; tell me where I am going wrong in that affair, and I will endeavour to go right. God knows I have striven to do my best for the girl, but, as you put matters, my best is very bad indeed.'

'Your best is as good as good can be, Ned, and if I have wounded you by speaking plainly, have I not wounded myself also? Are you not as dear to me as a son? Have I a thought or wish into which you do not enter? I want to see the old firm resuming the position it once held; I want to hear Desborne and Son spoken of as Desborne and Son were spoken of even in your grandfather's time, as it might have been now if——'

'If I had been a different man,' finished the Head of the Firm, with bitter emphasis.

'That is not what I was going to say,'

replied his uncle. ' All I will add now, however, is this : consider whether there is not
far too much truth in the opinion I have
expressed—harshly, if you choose to think
so.'

' There generally is some truth in any
opinion, provided it be disagreeable enough,'
answered Mr. Desborne, with a forced smile.

' It was not your better self which spoke
then, Ned,' returned his uncle.

' It was not—it was not,' acknowledged the
other eagerly. ' Forgive my petulance, but
you did hit so hard. I will think over what
you said. Is there ever anything you say to
which I fail to give respectful consideration ?
Tell me what you have in your mind about
Miss Fermoy, since the root of this dis-
cussion is to be found somewhere in connection with that matter.'

' Yes, because I do not want you to act
the Good Samaritan there to our disadvantage.
While benefiting her, it is surely not impossible to benefit ourselves. This is a critical
moment in our acquaintance with the girl; let
us make the most of it.'

'I am quite willing. What do you think ought to be done?'

'You heard Miss Simpson say that she had no fitting place in which to receive a pupil of any sort, more especially so exceptional a pupil as she supposed Miss Fermoy would be.'

'I did, and suggested, as you may remember, that she should hire apartments suitable for the purpose.'

'But Miss Simpson did not seem to take kindly to the idea.'

'No; she inclined to rent a house, and I think I can understand why. A house, however, can surely be found. It may take a little time to find one certainly, still———'

'There is a house—there are two houses ready to your hand,' interrupted Mr. Thomas Desborne.

'Where?'

'One belonging to Edward Desborne in York Street, and one belonging likewise to Edward Desborne called Ashwater. Edward Desborne cannot live in two houses at once;

therefore, when he is at Ashwater, Miss Simpson and her charge might well occupy his town residence, and when he returned to London Miss Simpson and Miss Fermoy could run down to Teddington and take possession for the winter of Ashwater, usually left to the tender and expensive mercies of a caretaker.'

Edward Desborne heard this programme with surprise, not to say dismay.

'I scarcely fancy that is an arrangement which Miss Simpson would care for,' he said, after a momentary pause.

'There I differ from you; it is one I imagine she would like very much. At all events, you can but mention what I have proposed. If my suggestion fail to recommend itself to her, of course there is an end of the matter.'

'And if she approved, I am quite certain my wife would not,' added Mr. Desborne, with conviction.

'Why?'

'It is difficult to explain, but I am satisfied she would object.'

'If the idea be properly put before her I cannot see why she should. It is not as though anyone were proposing that Miss Fermoy should reside with her; quite the contrary. By the plan I indicate Miss Simpson and her pupil will simply take the place of a care-taker. They will have the advantage of living in good, well-furnished houses, for which, if you like, you can charge a fair rent, and you will have the satisfaction of knowing you are making matters extremely easy for a client who is, I feel sure, a very good girl, and who will, there can be little doubt, prove a grateful one.'

The Head of the Firm sat silent for a short time. That his thoughts were not pleasant was evident from the expression of his face; nevertheless, at length he said:

'There is a good deal in your notion. It did not recommend itself to me at first, but—yes, there is much in its favour.'

'Then you will place it in as good a light as possible before Miss Simpson?'

Mr. Edward Desborne hesitated.

' Do you not think I ought first to speak to my wife ?'

' No ; whatever is done ought to be done this afternoon. If matters are arranged satisfactorily, I will tell Mrs. Desborne, should you wish me to do so.'

' I should not wish that ; I will explain everything to her myself.'

' Very well, then, I depend upon you, and —Ned—you are not vexed with me now, are you ?'

' No, only with myself. What a fool I have been !'

' Were I to say that, how angry you would be !'

' It is true, nevertheless ;' and the speaker walked out of the office and upstairs as if determined not to give himself time to change his mind.

' Well, am I too soon ?' he asked Miss Simpson, with a pleasant smile, which took in Aileen as well.

' Not at all ; we have finished our talk. I think I understand Miss Fermoy's wishes.'

' And you really are going to set up house together ?' he said, turning to his fortunate client.

' So Miss Simpson says,' answered the girl, as though she had no say at all in the matter.

' When I can find a suitable residence,' added Miss Simpson by way of rider.

' Do you know what my uncle suggests ?' said Mr. Desborne, in the assured tone of one who felt certain whatever his uncle suggested would be listened to with respectful attention.

' No ; pray tell me——'

' That you should live at York Street and Ashwater alternately ; that is, when we are in town he thinks you might reside at Ashwater, and when we are at Ashwater you might return to town.'

' Oh ! Mr. Desborne, do you really mean what you say ?'

' The idea is not disagreeable, then ?'

' Disagreeable ? Delightful ! the very thing ! the plan is perfect ! Who but Mr. Thomas Desborne would have thought of it ?'

'I should not, at all events,' returned the Head of the Firm, with frank truthfulness. 'You will like York Street, I know, and if you find Ashwater too dull, why, we can make some different arrangement.'

'Dear Ashwater! I should never feel dull there. I love it!' exclaimed Miss Simpson enthusiastically. 'But you, Miss Fermoy —perhaps such a home might seem too quiet. I did not think of that when I spoke.'

'You need not be afraid, ma'am,' replied Aileen tranquilly.

Was not 'quiet' what her soul and heart and body longed for? Could any place be too quiet for a girl who had lived in such a pandemonium as the double-fronted house in Field Prospect Road?

'It only seems too good to be true,' she murmured to herself softly; but Miss Simpson and Mr. Desborne caught the words, and ex-changed sympathetic glances.

'What do you think of her?' asked the lawyer half an hour later, as he conducted

Miss Simpson to a cab, Aileen lagging in her modest way behind.

'She has a lovely face,' was the answer.

'Which is but the index to a lovely nature,' he rejoined with confidence.

END OF VOL. I.

BILLING AND SONS, PRINTERS, GUILDFORD.